PLEASE DON'T
BE MINE,
JULIE VALENTINE!

Other Books by Todd Strasser

Help! I'm Trapped in My Teacher's Body

The Mall from Outer Space

The Diving Bell

Free Willy (novelization)

Home Alone™ (novelization)

Home Alone 2™ (novelization)

Beyond the Reef

The Complete Computer Popularity Program

Friends Till the End

PLEASE DON'T BE MINE, JULIE VALENTINE!

TODD STRASSER

AN
APPLE
PAPERBACK

SCHOLASTIC INC.
New York Toronto London Auckland Sydney

ISBN 0-590-48153-3

12 11 10 9 8 7 6 5 4 3 2 1   4 5 6 7 8 9/9

Printed in the U.S.A.   40

First Scholastic printing, January 1994

To Judy and Len

PLEASE DON'T BE MINE,
BE MINE,
JULIE VALENTINE!

1

"Hey, you gotta hear this." Gary Halkit held up the latest edition of the *Snorkwaller Snooper*. The headline said, "SPECIAL VALENTINE'S EDITION."

"Let me get this shot first," said Zack Warner. He was aiming an old camera at my tongue.

I waited with my mouth open and my tongue sticking out while Zack slowly adjusted the camera's focus. We were sitting at our regular table in the cafeteria at Snorkwaller Junior/Senior High.

"How long is this gonna take?" Gary asked impatiently. He was short and a little pudgy, with pale skin and wavy blond hair. People often thought he was still in grade school.

"Chill, my friend," Zack said. "I'm still trying to get all the little cracks and bumps in focus." A moment later he pressed a button and the camera went *click*!

"Got it." Zack put the camera down. He was

one of the tallest kids in seventh grade, and the only one who had started to shave. If Gary looked younger than he really was, then Zack was the exact opposite. He looked like a sophomore or maybe even a junior.

I closed my mouth. My tongue felt a little dry. With medium-length brown hair and a medium-size build, I looked pretty much the way you'd expect a seventh-grader to look.

"You guys ready now?" Gary asked.

"Sure."

"This week's guest editorial is by Julie Valentine, head cheerleader," he said.

"Ahhh, Julie." Zack pressed his hands together and stared at the ceiling as if he were praying. "Most beautiful and bodacious woman of my dreams."

Gary glanced out the corner of his eye at me. I just shrugged. Zack could be strange at times.

"Okay, listen," Gary said. "The editorial's called, 'Why I Believe in Valentine's Day.' "

"Kind of interesting that Julie Valentine is writing about Valentine's Day," I said.

"Makes perfect sense to me," said Zack.

Gary rustled the school newspaper. "Here's what she says: 'In recent years it appears that a lot of people have forgotten about Valentine's Day. They're either too busy to bother with it, or they think it's silly and old-fashioned. But closer to the truth is that they're probably afraid to let

2

their feelings show. I think that is really sad. Valentine's Day is important because it's the one day of the year when it's okay to express our feelings without anyone making fun of us. Instead of ignoring Valentine's Day we should use it to grow closer to the people we care about. In today's fast-paced world, it seems like there's less and less time for romance. Don't let romance die on this most romantic of all days. Ask someone to be your valentine.' "

"The perfect mixture of brains and beauty." Zack sighed.

"I wonder what Trey will think of it," I said. Trey Boice was Julie Valentine's boyfriend.

"The real question is, *does* Trey Boice think?" Zack asked.

"Why don't you ask him?" Gary nodded past us. Zack and I turned and saw Trey enter the cafeteria carrying a basketball under his arm. Six feet, four inches tall, and weighing around 225 pounds, he was a three-letter man and captain of the Snorkwaller Warriors. Adam Lampel and Jason Howard, both members of the basketball team, were with him. They were all wearing red-and-white team jackets.

Adam was holding a copy of the *Snooper* and giving Trey grief about it. "Hey, Trey, got anything romantic planned for Julie tomorrow?"

"Give me a break," Trey muttered.

"You mean, you're going to let romance die on

that most romantic of all days?" Jason kidded him.

"You're gonna die, too, if you don't shut up," Trey threatened. "Killer's been acting real cranky lately. I think he misses the taste of human flesh."

Adam and Jason chuckled nervously. The three of them headed down to the other end of the cafeteria where the senior high kids hung out.

"Who's Killer?" I asked.

"Trey's German shepherd," Gary said. "I heard he chewed up some guy who tried to get too friendly with Julie last year."

"Do you get the feeling that Trey doesn't think much of Valentine's Day?" Zack asked.

"I think Julie would be bummed if she heard that," I said.

"Maybe she'd even break up with him," Zack said hopefully.

"Get real," Gary said. "Trey's not only the best-looking athlete in the school, he's also one of the meanest guys around. If Julie broke up with him, you really think anyone would dare go out with her? Trey would sic Killer on them in an instant."

"Too bad." Zack's shoulders sagged. "For a second there I really had my hopes up."

"Think of it," I mused. "Julie Valentine going with a seventh-grader . . ."

"Dream on, guys." Gary crumpled his lunch bag into a ball. "So who thinks they can sink their lunch bag in the trash can from here?"

The open trash can stood beside the cafeteria door about twenty-five feet away.

"What happens if we miss?" I asked.

"You have to put two straws up your nose and walk backward to your next class," Zack suggested.

"That's grade school stuff," Gary said, irritably.

"Why don't we just see if we can sink our bags?" I asked. "Why does there always have to be some big dare attached?"

"You always say that because you know you're gonna miss," Gary taunted me.

"Will not," I said.

"Will too," said Gary. "Besides, if you're so sure you're going to make the shot, you shouldn't care what the dare is."

"Even Trey Boice misses a shot once in a while," I said. "And when he does, Coach Davis doesn't make him throw mashed potatoes at the cafeteria ceiling to see if they stick."

"Look, enough debate," Gary snapped. "This is very simple. You either sink your lunch bag in the garbage can or do the dare. Okay, Brett? You don't have to start chickening out before you even know what the dare is."

It was hard to argue against that kind of logic.

"Whoever misses has to see how many peas they can stick up their nose," Zack suggested.

Gary rolled his eyes. "Come on, Zack, we're in

junior high now. We gotta come up with something more mature than that."

"You don't want the high school kids to think we're immature seventh-graders, do you?" I asked jokingly, since that was pretty much what they thought of us.

"I want to come up with something good this time," Gary said. Zack and I waited as he scanned the crowded cafeteria for an idea. His eyes stopped at a big pink banner on the wall announcing the Valentine's Day dance the next night.

"That's it!" he said. "Whoever misses has to ask a girl to the dance."

"Naw, we did that for the Halloween costume ball, remember?" Zack said. "Brett had to take Beth Buford and she came dressed as a water buffalo."

"Oh, yea." Gary smiled at the memory. "Okay, then this time whoever misses doesn't have to ask a girl to the dance. He just has to ask her to be his valentine."

"*Any* girl?" Zack asked.

"No. . . ." Gary was staring at something behind us and a big grin curled across his lips. "Not just *any* girl."

2

Zack and I quickly turned around. Coming through the cafeteria entrance was Julie Valentine. She had long blonde hair, big brown eyes, and rosy cheeks. She held her head high when she walked, and her strides were long and natural. Her hair bounced lightly on her shoulders.

Julie didn't seem like she belonged at school. She looked like she belonged in a movie. We'd all seen photos of her in the local newspaper because she sometimes modeled for Miller's department store in town.

"Not Julie!" I gasped.

"Why not?" Gary asked, pointing to the *Snork-waller Snooper*. "Didn't she write about how important it is to ask someone to be your valentine?"

"Sounds good to me." Zack smiled at Julie as she came down the aisle toward us. Every day she passed us on her way to the other side of the cafeteria, leaving the scent of flowery perfume behind. Every day Zack smiled at her. But she never even looked at him.

"It's a really bad idea," I said.

"You chicken?" Gary whispered.

"No, but . . ."

"But what?" Gary asked. "We're all in this together. If I miss, I have to ask her. If one of you misses, you have to ask her."

"What about you-know-who?" I asked, pointing toward the other end of the cafeteria where Julie had joined Trey. He looked up and gave her a brief nod, then turned back to his buddies.

"That's the beauty of this dare," Gary said. "You really think Trey Boice is going to be jealous of one of *us*? Julie Valentine won't take it seriously. Some seventh-grader asking her to be his valentine? It'll just be a joke. Besides, all we have to say is we read her editorial."

It was at times like this that I regretted having Gary as a friend.

"So whoever misses has to go up to Julie tomorrow and ask her to be his valentine?" Zack asked.

"Well, they should give her a heart-shaped box of candy or something," Gary said. "I mean, you gotta do it right."

"Great." I grumbled. "Not only is this gonna be totally embarrassing, but it's gonna cost money as well."

"What are you so worried about?" Gary asked

8

me. "You could be the guy who sinks it on the first try."

"What happens if two of us miss?" Zack asked.

"We keep shooting until there's only one guy left," said Gary.

Word of the dare quickly spread to the tables around us. In no time a crowd of kids was watching and cheering us on. Gary went first. His shot fell short, and I felt a little better. Even if I missed on my first try, I'd get a second chance.

Zack went next. His shot went wide to the right and landed on the cafeteria floor.

I went last. My crumpled lunch bag felt good leaving my hand. The aim was dead on. I held my breath. The bag hit the rim of the garbage can . . . and fell to the floor. The kids around me groaned.

"Nice try, Brett."

"Too bad, man."

"See, Brett? You were the closest." Gary walked over to the garbage can and came back with our crumpled bags.

"Round two," someone said.

Gary went first again.

Swoosh. His bag sank squarely in the can. A couple of kids clapped. Gary raised his fist and gave us a big grin. Zack and I gave each other unhappy looks. One of us was going to ask Julie to be our valentine tomorrow.

Zack went again and missed. Now it was my

turn. I took aim and shot. *Darn!* As soon as the bag left my hand, I felt it going wide.

"Round three!" Gary cried cheerfully as he picked up our bags. He could afford to be happy. No matter what happened, he wouldn't have to ask Julie to be his valentine.

Zack took aim again and launched a high one. It was going to miss by a mile. Suddenly Mr. Grooms, the janitor, walked past, pushing a bucket and mop. Zack's bag bounced off Mr. Grooms's head and fell into the trash can.

"Huh?" Mr. Grooms looked around and scratched his head.

"No fair!" I yelled.

"Why not?" Zack asked.

"It bounced off his head!"

"So? I banked it in," Zack said.

"That's interference," I insisted.

"What's the call, Gary?" Zack asked.

Gary rubbed his chin. "Let's ask Mr. Grooms."

We crowded around him. Mr. Grooms had a big stomach, a thick mustache, and a greasy brown ponytail. He was always sweating, even on the coldest winter days. Gary explained how Zack's lunch bag had bounced off his head and into the garbage can.

Mr. Grooms patted his forehead with his handkerchief. "Tell you the truth, boys. I don't care how the garbage gets in the can as long as it gets there."

10

"Yes!" Zack pumped his fist.

"I guess that means it counts." Gary said.

"But it's really not over," Zack said. "I had three turns and Brett only had two. So Brett really should get one more shot."

"Go, Brett, go!" the crowd chanted. "Go, Brett, go!"

I picked up my bag and tried to picture the shot in my mind like the pros do. But instead of imagining the bag going into the trash can, all I saw was Julie Valentine looking at me as if I'd lost my mind.

I shot my bag. It arced high through the air and hit the garbage can rim just like my first shot had . . . then fell to the floor.

"Hey, too bad." Zack patted me on the back.

"Congratulations, Brett," Gary said with a grin. "Tomorrow, you get to ask Julie to be your valentine."

"I still say it's not fair."

"Hey, what can I tell you?" Gary shrugged. "All's fair in love and war."

3

Every day after school I picked up my sister, Nicole, at Peabody Elementary and walked her home. We'd recently moved to a new house. Now we lived too close to take the bus, but just far enough away that our parents didn't want Nicole to walk home alone even though she was in the fourth grade. Our parents both worked and they liked knowing that I was around the house with Nicole in the afternoon.

Nicole's favorite color was lavender, and that day she was wearing a dark lavender parka and lighter lavender jeans. She was carrying a lavender backpack filled with books. She even had lavender clips in her short brown hair.

"What's bugging you?" she asked as we walked down the sidewalk.

"Nothing."

"Then how come you're in such a bad mood?"

"Who said I was in a bad mood?"

"Oh, come on, Brett," she said. "You're acting

like you have a big dark cloud hanging over your head."

I waved my hand over my head as if to sweep the cloud away. "There, it's gone."

"Nope, it's still there," Nicole said.

"No, it isn't."

"Let me guess," Nicole said. "You let that jerk, Gary Halkit, talk you into another stupid dare."

I gave her a surprised glance.

"I knew it!" She grinned.

"You think you're so smart," I muttered.

"Matter of fact, I do," Nicole replied smugly. "When are you going to stop letting him trick you into doing dumb things?"

"He didn't trick me," I said. "He could have gotten stuck with the dare just as easily as me."

"That's what you always say, but does it ever happen?" she asked. "Noooooo."

I shrugged. "He's just lucky."

"Lucky?" Nicole shook her head and her short brown hair swung back and forth. "When are you going to wake up and smell the coffee, Brett? Gary's not lucky. He only picks dares he knows he can win. I bet he's never suggested a dare based on who could jump the highest."

"That wouldn't be fair," I said. "Zack and I are taller than him."

"That's just my point," Nicole said. "So what was the dare this time?"

13

"Who could shoot their lunch bags into the garbage can from twenty-five feet."

"Are you crazy?" Nicole stared at me.

"What are you talking about? I'm a good shot."

"You can't even hit the backboard from the free throw line half the time," Nicole said. "Meanwhile, what's Gary doing every time you go to his house?"

"Shooting baskets," I admitted glumly.

"So what did he dare you to do this time?"

"It's no big deal," I said. "I just have to ask this girl to be my valentine."

"Who? The water buffalo?"

"No. Someone else."

"A girl in your class?"

"No."

"Of course not," Nicole said. "Knowing Gary, he'll probably make you ask some eighth-grader."

I shook my head.

"Ninth?"

"Nope."

"Tenth?" Nicole screwed up her face in disbelief.

"Worse."

"*A junior?*"

"A senior," I said regretfully.

Nicole stopped on the sidewalk and stared at me. "You, a lowly seventh-grader, are going to ask a *senior* to be your valentine?"

"It's worse than that."

"How can it be worse than that?"

"It's not just any girl. It's Julie Valentine."

"Who?"

"The girl in the Miller's department store ads."

"The one with the tall, handsome boyfriend who's like All-County everything?" Nicole asked.

"That's the one."

My sister shook her head in disbelief. "Say your prayers, Brett."

"Don't be so dramatic," I said. "It's just gonna be a dumb joke. No one's gonna take it seriously."

"You better hope not," Nicole warned.

We'd only been living in our new house since late August. It was bigger than our old house and had a lot more lawn around it for me to mow. Mom and Dad bought the new house because they were having so much success with their business, Cross-County Glass and Mirror. Dad ran the business and Mom ran the office. They were so busy it seemed like they were hardly ever home.

The only strange thing about where we lived was the house next door — this old, dark mansion that Nicole and I passed every day going to and from school. A tall brick wall surrounded the mansion, and the lawn was overgrown with weeds. Now that it was winter, everything looked dead and brown.

The mansion itself was pretty rundown. A lot of the windows were broken. Some were covered with plastic. Shutters hung at angles and creaked in the wind, and part of the porch roof sagged. An old sign next to the iron gate across the driveway said, E. N. CHANTER. Nicole and I assumed Mr. Chanter was the old man with long white hair we sometimes saw from our bedroom windows. He spent most of his time in this big, old greenhouse behind the mansion. Sometimes when we were out in our backyard, we would hear loud laughter coming from the greenhouse, but we never saw anyone except the white-haired man.

"Look," Nicole said as we turned the corner onto our street and started to pass the mansion. "The gate's open. Want to take a peek?"

"No way," I said.

"Aren't you curious?" Nicole asked.

"No."

"Bull."

"Okay, maybe a little curious," I admitted. "But not curious enough to trespass."

"Oh, come on, Brett. We're too young to be trespassers. At our age we can always get away with being foolishly curious. Besides, the big black car that's always in the driveway is gone. He must be out."

"What's the point?" I asked.

"I want to see what the place looks like," Nicole said. "We're not going to break into the house or anything. We'll just look around."

"Sorry, Nicole. I'm not interested. Besides, I have a big science test to study for."

"Chicken."

I stopped and stared at her. "Aren't you the one who just yelled at me for taking stupid dares?"

"I'm not daring you to do anything," Nicole said. "I just want you to come with me."

"Sounds to me like *you're* the chicken if you won't go alone," I said.

"You're right," Nicole said. "I'm a great big chicken. Now please come with me?"

"No."

"I'll shovel the driveway the next time it snows," she said.

"Promise?"

"Double promise."

"And I get to pick the TV shows we watch this week?"

"Oh, okay," Nicole agreed reluctantly. "That, too."

"Deal."

4

We slipped inside the gate and looked around. Tall pine trees lined the driveway leading to the mansion. You couldn't really tell where the driveway ended and the lawn began because the ground was covered by a thick layer of dry brown pine needles. As we walked toward the house, we could see that the porch steps were broken and the porch itself was missing planks. The windows were covered with tattered shades. It looked dark and creepy inside.

"What do you think?" Nicole asked in a low voice.

"It really needs a paint job," I said.

"Let's go around the back."

I followed her through the dead brown brush and weeds to the back of the house. There was an old swimming pool, but it was empty and cracked, and the diving board was missing.

"Brett!" Nicole whispered. "Come look!"

She was pressing her face against the greenhouse, which stood between the pool and the mansion. The greenhouse also had lots of cracked and broken windows covered with plastic. The glass was foggy, and it was difficult to see inside.

"Dad could make a fortune replacing the glass in this place," I whispered.

"Look inside," Nicole said.

I tried to squint through the windows, but all I could see were splotches of bright colors. "What?"

"Those flowers are incredible," Nicole said.

"How do you know they're flowers?"

"What else could they be?" Nicole began to work her way around the side of the greenhouse.

Creak! From somewhere in the mansion came the sound of a door opening.

"I think we ought to go," I said, looking around nervously.

"Why?"

"Because we're not supposed to be here, and this place gives me the creeps."

"Just a minute."

Click!

I heard a metallic sound. "What was that?"

"The door," Nicole said.

"What are you doing?" I gasped.

"I want to see the flowers," Nicole said. "Come on."

The greenhouse door squeaked as Nicole pushed it open. A cloud of moist, pungent air billowed into my face as I stepped in behind her.

"This is a really bad idea, Nicole."

"I just want to look," she said. "I promise I won't stay more than a minute."

I followed her inside the greenhouse. It felt like it was ninety degrees. Long pink lights hung from chains on the ceiling. A strong scent hung in the air. "What's that smell?"

"I think it's fertilizer and flowers." Nicole looked around. "These plants are amazing. I've never seen anything like them."

There were hundreds of plants and flowers — on broad, flat tables in the middle of the greenhouse, and on tall shelves lining the glass walls.

"Maybe they're from other countries," I said.

"Look at this!" She pointed at a dark green plant with half a dozen large purple flowers growing from thorny stems. The flowers were the deepest purple I'd ever seen. Like something out of a Walt Disney cartoon.

Nicole bent down and took a deep sniff. She staggered backward.

"What's wrong?" I asked.

My sister gave me a blank look. Her eyes were suddenly glazed.

"Nicole?"

She shook her head and blinked. "Wow. I don't know what that is, but it's really strong."

Creak! From somewhere outside came the sound of another door swinging.

"Let's get out of here, okay?" I said. "You've seen the flowers and they're really nice, but now it's time to go."

I expected Nicole to give me an argument. After all, she nearly always did. So I was really surprised when she simply nodded and said, "You're right, Brett."

We left the greenhouse and started back along the side of the mansion. Suddenly, I heard the sound of a car.

"It must be him!"

"Who?" Nicole asked behind me.

"Mr. Chanter."

Nicole didn't look worried. Instead she gazed dreamily at me. "Did I ever tell you how good you look in a blue turtleneck?"

"Huh? Are you crazy? Come on." I turned around and headed toward the backyard. The brick wall around Mr. Chanter's property was about eight feet tall. Ahead of us was a tree growing close to the wall. I had an idea.

"Let's climb the tree," I said. "Maybe we'll be able to get over the wall."

"What a brilliant idea," Nicole said behind me. I assumed she was being sarcastic. I mean, she *never* said stuff like that.

We reached the tree. "I'll go up and see if we can do it," I said.

"So brave," said Nicole wistfully.

I scowled at her, then quickly climbed up the tree. By holding onto a large branch, I was able to step on top of the wall.

"It worked!" I called down to her. "Come on, hurry!"

Nicole climbed up the tree. I held her hand and helped her onto the wall. It was a long way down on the other side. I kneeled down and lowered myself as far as I could, then let go and dropped the rest of the way.

"Okay," I said. "You do it and I'll catch you."

Nicole lowered herself down the side of the wall and let go. I tried to catch her. It had been a long time since I'd picked up my sister and she must have grown, because we both tumbled to the ground and lay there for a moment.

"My hero!" Without any warning, Nicole threw her arms around my neck and hugged me.

"Back off!" I pulled away. "What's wrong with you?"

Nicole looked upset. "Don't you like me?"

"Get a grip," I said. "You're my sister. You never hug me."

"Oh." Nicole looked disappointed. She stood up and brushed herself off. We walked across our backyard and went into our house through the sliding kitchen door.

Nicole stopped in the kitchen and took off her parka. "Want to do something?"

"Like what?" I asked.

"I don't know. Whatever you want."

I stared at her. "What's with you?"

Nicole shrugged. "Nothing."

"Every day we do the same thing," I said. "We get home from school and do our homework. Then we have dinner and clean up. Then we watch TV until Mom and Dad get home. Then we go to bed."

"Want to do homework together?" she asked.

"We *never* do homework together," I said. "Besides, if I don't study for that science test, I'm gonna be in big trouble."

"Oh." Nicole pouted as if I'd hurt her feelings. Then she picked up her backpack and left the kitchen. I swear, sometimes she acted like a real nut job.

5

I don't know what had gotten into my sister the day before, but by the next morning she was her normal annoying self again. Our parents usually left for work before we got up, but this morning they were late.

"Brett, please take something out of the freezer for tonight," Mom said as she quickly sipped her coffee.

Meanwhile, Dad was tying his tie while he cradled the phone against his ear. "That's right," he said. "I need a crew at the hardware store on Palmer. Someone broke their window last night."

Mom finished making notes just about the same time Dad got off the phone. She kissed Nicole on the cheek and rubbed my head. "Have a good day at school."

"Stay out of trouble," said Dad.

My sister and I watched them hurry out of the house. Nicole had already started her breakfast. She was sitting at the kitchen table with a bowl of Sugar Pops, a big glass of milk, and the newspaper spread out. I poured some Sugar Pops into a bowl and opened the refrigerator.

"Hey, where's the milk?"

"It's all gone," Nicole said.

"You mean, you used it all," I said, slamming the refrigerator door.

"First come, first served."

"Thanks a lot," I said irritably. "For a second yesterday I thought you'd changed. Boy, was I wrong."

"I never changed for an instant," Nicole said.

"Oh, yeah? You didn't say my escape plan was brilliant? You didn't call me your hero and hug me?"

"Hug *you*?" Nicole stuck out her tongue and made a face. "That's the grossest thing I ever heard."

"But you did," I said.

"Did not," said my sister.

"Did too."

"You're crazy," Nicole said. Then she pointed at the newspaper. "Anyway, here's your girl-friend."

I looked over her shoulder and saw a full-page photo of Julie Valentine in a bathing suit.

"She's not my girlfriend," I said.

"You just wish she was."

"Do not."

"Do too."

The phone rang.

"You gonna answer it?" I asked.

Nicole shook her head. "You get it. It's probably Mom changing her mind about dinner."

I answered the phone. "Hello?"

"Hey, Brett." It was Gary. "Don't forget what day it is."

"Believe me, I don't need to be reminded."

"Did you get a heart-shaped box of candy for Julie?" Gary asked.

"Sorry, I forgot."

"Hey, come on, dude, that was part of the deal, remember?"

"Well, it's not part of the deal anymore," I said.

"You gotta give her something," Gary said. "It's tradition. You can't just walk up to a girl and ask her to be your valentine without giving her a token of your affection."

"Just watch me."

"I'm serious," Gary said. "You gotta give her something. The whole grade knows about this, man. You don't want to look like a jerk, do you?"

"I'm going to look like a jerk no matter what."

"Maybe, but you can be a jerk with class, or you can be a jerk with no class," Gary said. "Besides, for all we know, Trey Boice may think it's a real insult for some seventh-grader to ask Julie to be his valentine and not give her anything."

"Sure, Gary. See you later." I hung up.

"What was that about?" Nicole asked.

"If you were going to ask someone to be your valentine, do you really think you'd have to give her something, too?" I asked.

"Well, that's the way it's always been done," Nicole said.

"Great." I groaned and slumped into a chair. "There's no way I'll have time to get a heart-shaped box of candy. We have to be in school in twenty minutes."

"Give her flowers," Nicole suggested.

"Where am I going to get flowers in the middle of win — " I had an idea. "Wait a minute!"

"What?" Nicole asked.

I pulled open one of the kitchen drawers and took out a scissors. Then I grabbed some newspaper. "Be right back."

I knew what I was going to do wasn't honest or right, but I was desperate. Besides, if you cut a flower off a plant, another one eventually grows to take its place. I figured with so many flowers in the greenhouse, Mr. Chanter probably wouldn't even notice if I took a few.

Outside, I put a ladder against the wall opposite the tree we'd climbed the day before. In no time I was over the wall and shimmying down the tree. Moments later, in the greenhouse, I carefully snipped one orange flower, one blue, one red, one yellow, one pink, and one of those big purple flowers Nicole had sniffed the day before. Taking care not to prick myself on the thorny stems, I wrapped them in the newspaper and went back home.

"I can't believe you stole them," Nicole said as I left the flowers on the kitchen counter and went to find some wrapping paper.

"I didn't steal them," I shouted from the den. "I borrowed them."

"Oh? And I suppose you're going to return them?"

"Okay, okay, I know it was wrong," I said as I rushed back into the kitchen with the wrapping paper. "I swear I'll never do anything like this again. But Gary didn't leave me any choice. I have to give Julie *something* when I ask her to be my valentine."

"I just hope she appreciates them," Nicole said.

"Believe me," I said. "She won't."

6

From the moment I walked into school, kids razzed me about asking Julie to be my valentine. Gary was right, everyone knew. This was probably going to be the single most humiliating thing I'd ever done, but I was a man of my word and a dare was a dare.

I left the flowers in my locker all morning. We had the science test and I knew I did pretty badly. The night before, I'd been so distracted by my "Julie problem" that it was hard to study.

Just before lunch I stopped at my locker to get the flowers. I had to ask Julie in the cafeteria because that was the only place where I was sure to see her. Sometimes we passed in the hall, but I couldn't count on it.

I was taking the flowers out of my locker when Gary and Zack appeared on either side of me. Zack pointed his camera at me and took a picture.

"What are you doing?" I asked.

"We need pictures so that someday we can look back at this and laugh," Zack said.

"Thanks a lot." I slammed the locker door closed.

Gary slid his hand around my arm.

"Now what?" I asked.

"I just want to make sure you get to the cafeteria safely," he said.

"Why?" I asked. "Did you think I'll chicken out?"

"Yes."

"Well, you're wrong." I pulled my arm away. "I said I'd do it, and I will."

It seemed like half the cafeteria was waiting for us when Gary, Zack, and I came through the doors. We sat down at our regular table, but I hardly touched my peanut-butter-and-jelly sandwich.

"Lost your appetite?" Gary asked with a wink.

"Don't look so happy," I said. "I thought you were supposed to be my friend."

"I *am* your friend," Gary insisted. "And I'm proud of your courage and fortitude."

"Just remind me not to accept another dare from you for as long as I live," I said.

"Which may not be very long," Zack added.

Julie Valentine always got to the cafeteria late. As the minutes ticked away, I could feel my throat grow tight and my mouth go dry.

The cafeteria doors opened and Julie Valentine stepped in. She stopped and scowled slightly when she saw how quiet it was, and how all the junior high kids were looking at her. Then she began to walk down the aisle toward our table.

Gary nudged me in the ribs with his elbow. "Go!"

It was hard to breathe. My heart was beating so fast it felt like it might break loose in my chest.

Gary jabbed me a little harder. "Go on," he whispered.

I took a deep breath and got up slowly. My legs felt rubbery. I could hear kids murmuring behind me. Everything felt like slow motion as I walked toward the aisle. Julie didn't even notice me. She was probably looking for Trey.

I stepped into the aisle and held up the bouquet of flowers.

Click! Out of the corner of my eye, I saw Zack take a picture.

"Uh, er, excuse me," I stammered. I must have been blushing pretty hard because my face felt like it was burning.

Julie stopped and looked down at me with a puzzled expression.

"Will, uh, you be my valentine?" I asked, handing her the flowers.

The whole junior high side of the cafeteria was silent, waiting for Julie's reaction. She glanced

31

around and the slightest smile appeared on her face, as if she suddenly understood what was going on.

"How sweet," she said, "and what beautiful flowers."

She reached for the flowers.

"Ouch!"

The next thing I knew, she pulled her finger away. I caught a glimpse of blood on her fingertip before she pressed it against her lips. She must have pricked her finger on a thorn from the stem of the purple flower.

"Oh, gee, I'm sorry!" I gasped. "I didn't mean for you to get pricked. Really."

Julie nodded. When she looked at me again, her eyes were sort of glassy.

"Who . . . who are you?" she asked.

"Uh, Brett Bergen."

Julie gazed at me with a dreamy expression on her face. The same way Nicole had looked at me the day before.

"Brett," she repeated, barely louder than a whisper.

"Look, I'm really sorry," I said. "If you want, I can go down to the nurse's office and get you a Band-Aid."

"No, it's okay. . . . I'll be fine." She smiled at me. "Brett. . . . I like that name."

"You do?"

"Julie?" a voice said.

I turned around. Trey Boice was standing behind me. I'm not sure he even saw me.

"Come on," he said, taking her hand. "The photos of the basketball team just came in. There's a really good one of me you have to see."

He led Julie away. A second later I felt a hand on my shoulder. It was Gary.

"Nice going, Ace," he said. "You couldn't offer her flowers without thorns?"

"Hey, it wasn't my fault," I said, looking down at the flowers I was still holding. "At least I asked her." I turned back toward our table where my lunch sat, untouched. Now that the ordeal was over, my appetite was starting to come back. I put the flowers down and began to eat. Gary and Zack sat with me.

"Well, that turned out to be a great big nothing," Gary grumbled. The rest of the kids in the cafeteria must have thought so, too, because they'd gone back to doing normal stuff like shouting and having food fights.

"That's life," I said as I bit into my sandwich. "I did the dare. That's what counts."

Gary suddenly brightened. "What do you say we jump on ketchup packets and see whose squirts the farthest."

"I'll pass," I said.

"Me, too," said Zack.

"You guys are no fun," Gary muttered.

"So what's going on tonight?" Zack asked.

"The Valentine's Day dance," I said.

"We could check it out," Gary said.

"What's the point?" Zack asked. "You know what always happens. The junior high girls stand on one side of the cafeteria and the boys stand on the other. The only ones who dance are the high school kids."

"At least it's free," Gary said. "So if it's really bogus we can always leave."

Zack turned to me. "What do you think, Brett?"

"I guess it can't hurt," I said.

We agreed to meet outside the gym at eight o'clock. Then the bell rang and it was time to go to our next class. As I picked up my books, I glanced across the cafeteria. Down at the senior high end, Julie Valentine also stood up. She smiled and waved. I looked behind me to see if there was someone else she was waving at. But there wasn't. She was waving at me.

7

Nicole was having a sleepover at her friend
Gwen's that night, and Mom asked me to
drop her off on my way to the dance.

"Did you ask the Miller's department store girl
to be your valentine?" my sister asked as we
walked along the dark sidewalk. It was cold out
and our breaths were long, white plumes.

"Yeah."

"What happened?"

"It was kind of a dud. She pricked her finger
on one of the thorns. Then her boyfriend came
and they left."

"What are you doing tonight?" Nicole asked.

"Going to the Valentine's Day dance."

"Are you taking anyone?"

"Get serious," I said. "Nobody takes anyone in
seventh grade. Everyone just shows up and stares
at each other for a while, then they leave."

"Sounds incredibly exciting," Nicole said.

I dropped her off and went over to the school.

I was a little early, so I waited outside the gym entrance for Gary and Zack.

"Brett?" Someone called my name. I turned around. Julie Valentine was walking toward me.

"Oh, uh, hi," I said, swallowing nervously.

"Hi." Julie gave me that dreamy look again. She was wearing Trey Boice's team jacket and a tight black skirt. Her wavy blonde hair tumbled down over her shoulders. I could smell her perfume.

"So, uh, how's your finger?" I asked.

"It's okay."

"I'm really sorry about that," I said. "It really was an accident."

"I'm sure it was, Brett." Julie smiled softly. "I know you're not the kind of person who would do something like that on purpose."

How did she know that? I wondered.

"What grade are you in?" she asked.

"Uh, seventh."

"Really?" Julie seemed surprised. "You seem so mature for your age."

"I do?" No one had ever said *that* to me before.

Julie nodded. I felt kind of funny standing outside the school, talking to her. Kids were giving us looks as they went into the gym. I knew what they were thinking: *What's she talking to him for?*

Frankly, I was feeling the same way.

"Are you waiting for your date?" Julie asked.

Before I could answer, Trey Boice stepped out

of the shadows. "The car's parked," he said. "Let's go in."

He put his arm around Julie's shoulder and led her inside. Once again, I was pretty sure he hadn't even noticed me. As they left, Julie glanced over her shoulder at me and smiled.

"What was that all about?" Gary asked, coming up the sidewalk.

"What?"

"You were talking to Julie Valentine."

"So?"

"*You* and Julie Valentine?"

"What's so strange about that?"

"I'll tell you what's strange about it," Gary said. "We've been at this school for five-and-a-half months and I've never seen Julie Valentine talk to anyone less than a junior."

"People change, I guess."

"What did you talk about?" Gary asked.

"Nothing much. Just her finger." I decided not to mention the stuff about her saying how mature I was, since that was bound to get a laugh.

"Seemed like you talked about her finger for an awful long time," Gary said. "You sure you didn't talk about anything else?"

"Well, she did ask if I was waiting for my date," I said.

Gary's jaw dropped.

"What's so strange about that?" I asked. "She was probably just curious."

"What are you guys arguing about now?" Zack asked, joining us.

Gary told him about finding Julie and me talking.

"Interesting," Zack said.

"Not really," I said.

"I dare you to talk to her again," Gary said.

"Drop dead, Gary. I'm tired of you and your dares."

Gary turned to Zack. "Brett's acting a little touchy. Maybe he has a crush on her."

"Get lost," I said. "She must be five or six years older than me."

"So?"

"So she was just being friendly," I said. "Now let's go inside."

The inside of the gym was decorated with pink and red streamers. The walls were covered with big red hearts and flowers. At one end of the gym a band was playing, and at the other end were long tables with large bowls of red and pink punch.

Zack, Gary, and I hung our coats on racks and went in. Crowds of kids were standing around. All the junior high kids were down at our end and all the senior high kids were at the other end. Sort of like lunch, only without the tables.

I looked at the end of the gym where the high school kids were. Trey Boice and a bunch of guys from the basketball team were with their girlfriends. I noticed that Julie Valentine wasn't really talking to anyone. Instead, she was glancing . . . at me!

I quickly turned away.

When I looked back, her eyes met mine. Then she smiled and winked.

I turned around fast. "Uh, maybe we should go."

"What's with you?" Gary asked.

"I don't think anything interesting's gonna happen here."

"Give it time," Gary said. "Hey, look, there's Mr. Arnold."

Mr. Arnold, our science teacher, was standing near the band. He was wearing thick glasses and an ugly plaid jacket, which meant he was a chaperon.

"I wonder if he's corrected the science tests yet," Gary said.

"Let's go ask," said Zack.

I already knew how I'd done on the science test — miserably. So while Zack and Gary went to talk to Mr. Arnold, I went over to the refreshment table and poured myself a paper cup of punch.

When I turned around, I found Julie Valentine standing right behind me.

8

How's the punch?" she asked.
"Uh, okay." I quickly looked around. Zack and Gary were chatting with Mr. Arnold. Trey Boice was busy talking to his basketball buddies.

"Would you pour me a cup?" Julie asked.

"Oh, uh, sure." I poured her a cup and handed it to her.

Julie took a sip and smiled coyly at me. "Aren't dances funny? Everyone just stands around, waiting for someone else to start dancing."

"I bet you and Trey could get everyone dancing," I said.

"Trey hates to dance," Julie said. "All he ever wants to do is talk to his friends about sports."

"Well, that's kind of understandable," I said nervously. "I mean, he is the best athlete at school."

"Don't you think there's more to life than sports?" Julie asked.

"Uh, well, sure," I said. "There's video games and pizza and skateboards and stuff like that."

Julie laughed. "I didn't know you had such a sense of humor, Brett."

Neither did I, I thought. *I was serious.*

"Well, what do *you* think there is besides sports?" I asked.

Julie put down her cup and stepped close to me. Her eyes seemed to sparkle as she spoke. "I think there are relationships, Brett. Relationships between people who truly care about each other, people who are on the same wavelength. I think there are people who are meant to be together despite their age or grade, because their feelings for each other transcend all artificial boundaries. Don't you agree?"

"Uh. . . ." Not only was I not sure if I agreed, I wasn't even sure what she'd *said*. The only thing I was sure of was that it was weird for Julie Valentine to be talking like that to me.

"Hey, Julie, I've been looking all over for you." Trey Boice moved between Julie and me, stepping on my foot in the process. "How's the punch?"

His heel was crushing my toe, and no matter how hard I tried, I couldn't pull my foot away. Finally, I tapped him on the back. He turned and looked surprised to see me there. "What do you want, kid?"

"Excuse me, but you're crushing my foot," I said.

41

Trey moved his foot and slid his arm around Julie's waist. "So listen," he said as he led her away. "You never told me which of my pictures you liked the best."

Julie allowed herself to be guided away, but she gazed back over her shoulder at me. She looked unhappy and moved her lips silently. I'm not a great lip reader, but I could have sworn she mouthed the word *later*.

Just then I felt a hand clamp down on my shoulder and spin me around. Gary and Zack stared at me with wondrous expressions.

"What was *that* all about?" Gary asked, pressing his face close to mine.

"Nothing."

"Don't give me that," Gary said. "What's going on between you and Julie Valentine?"

"I don't know."

Gary glanced at Zack.

"Well, what were you talking about?" Zack asked.

"And don't tell us it was her finger," Gary added.

"Just things," I said.

Gary grabbed my shirt. "Cut it out, Brett. I'm serious. You guys were talking. Now what gives?"

"None of your business," I said, pushing his hands away, and smoothing out my shirt. "We were just talking, that's it."

Gary pursed his lips and looked really mad. "Look, if you don't tell us," he said, making a fist.

"What're you gonna do about it?" I asked, sticking my chin out.

Zack quickly stepped between us and spoke to Gary. "Okay, wait a minute. It's stupid to fight about this. Brett has a right not to tell us if he doesn't want to." Then he turned to me. "On the other hand, we *are* your best friends, Brett. I'm sure Gary would tell you if something like this happened to him."

"Yeah," Gary said with a pout.

"Oh, okay," I said. "You really want to know what we talked about?"

Gary and Zack nodded eagerly.

"She asked me if I thought there was more to life than sports, so I told her what I thought. Then she started talking about relationships, and people being on the same wavelength, and transcending artificial boundaries."

Gary frowned and picked up the half-finished cup of punch Julie had left on the refreshment table. He sniffed it, then held it under Zack's nose. "What does that smell like to you?"

Zack took a sniff. "Punch."

"That's what I thought, too," Gary said, putting the cup down. "Look, Brett, Julie Valentine doesn't talk to seventh-graders. She doesn't even know they *exist*. Now every time I turn around she's talking to you. It doesn't make sense."

43

"Not to *you* maybe," I said.

"What are you talking about?" Gary asked.

"Did it ever occur to you that maybe Julie Valentine is tired of guys who just stand around all the time talking to their friends?" I asked.

"But that's all we ever do," Zack said.

"Yeah, but we don't just talk about sports," I said.

Gary looked at me as if I were crazy. "What is this leading to?"

I took a deep breath and let it out slowly. "Well, all I'm saying is, maybe she likes me."

Gary and Zack looked at each other with stunned expressions on their faces.

"You've really lost it, Brett," Gary said. "I mean, if that's what you think, then you're in need of some serious — "

"Uh, Gary?" Zack tapped him on the shoulder and nodded toward the other side of the gym at Trey and Julie. Trey was talking to his friends again. Julie was gazing at me again. This time I didn't look away.

"She's staring at us," Gary whispered.

"Not *us*." Zack pointed at me. "*Him*."

"I don't believe it," Gary gasped.

"It's like there's no one else in the gym except Brett," Zack whispered.

Julie raised her hand and gave me a sad wave. This time Trey noticed and started to look in our direction.

"Quick!" Zack hissed. We instantly spun around so our backs faced him.

"Think he saw us?" Gary whispered.

"I don't think so," I whispered back.

Gary looked up and peeked over his shoulder. "He's still over there. I think we better go."

"Good idea," Zack said.

The three of us headed toward the exit. As we went through the door, I glanced back inside. Julie was still watching me.

We got our coats and went outside. A moment later we stood under the outdoor lights, watching our breaths curl into the cold February air. For a while, no one said anything.

Finally, Gary said, "That was weird."

"Amazing," said Zack.

"What are we gonna do?" Gary asked.

"What do you mean *we*?" I asked. "What does it have to do with you?"

"I feel responsible," Gary said. "After all, it was my idea that you should ask her to be your valentine."

"Maybe it was your idea," I said. "But I'm the one she was staring at."

"Yeah, but I dared you," Gary said. "If it wasn't for me, she wouldn't even know you existed."

"Did anyone ever tell you that you're totally conceited?" I asked.

"Me?!" Gary yelled. "You're the one who thinks Julie Valentine has a crush on you."

"Well, maybe she does," I shouted back.

"Oh, yeah!" Gary laughed haughtily. "And maybe I'm Arnold Schwarzenegger!"

"Drop it, guys," Zack said calmly. "This is a totally ridiculous argument. We should be happy for you, Brett. There are probably a million guys who wish Julie Valentine would pay as much attention to them as she does to you. You should feel honored."

"See?" I said to Gary.

But Gary just smirked.

"What's so funny?" Zack asked.

"Brett's going to be honored, all right," Gary said. "At his funeral."

"What are you talking about?" I asked.

"I'm talking about what's going to happen when Trey Boice finds out that his girlfriend likes some seventh-grader better than she likes him."

I gave Zack a nervous glance.

"Get real, Gary," said Zack. "There's a big difference between Julie just talking to Brett and her breaking up with Trey because of him."

Gary turned to me. "You better hope he's right."

46

9

The next morning I was eating breakfast when Nicole came into the kitchen. Today she was actually wearing a white blouse. But over it was a vest with lavender flowers.

"How was the big dance?" she asked as she poured Sugar Pops into a bowl.

"Okay," I said.

"Just okay?"

"Actually, it was pretty interesting," I said.

"How come?"

"Julie Valentine talked to me."

"Who?"

"The Miller's department store girl."

"The one you asked to be your valentine?"

"Yup."

"So?"

"So she's the most beautiful, popular girl at school. Girls like that don't talk to guys like me."

Nicole poured milk over her Sugar Pops. "Has

47

anyone ever told you that you have a bad self-image?"

"This has nothing to do with self-image," I said. "It has to do with . . . uh, it's like a pecking order. She's at the top of the heap and I'm at the bottom. She's like the queen and I'm just some peasant. It's like we're from two different worlds."

"People from different worlds can talk to each other."

"Not about the stuff we talked about," I said.

"Like what?"

"Like about having relationships, and about people liking each other even though they're different ages and in different grades. I mean, she acted like she really liked me."

Nicole gave me a funny look. "Brett, are you saying that the most popular, beautiful, senior girl at school likes *you*?"

I nodded.

"I take back what I said before," my sister said. "You don't have a bad self-image. You've just gone psycho."

"If you had seen the way Julie looked at me last night, you wouldn't say that."

"It doesn't make any sense, Brett."

"You think *I* don't know that?" I asked. "It doesn't make any sense to me either. I'm just telling you how it is."

"Right." Nicole responded with an exaggerated nod.

48

"Okay, fine," I said. "Don't believe me. See if I care."

It was a mild, sunny day for February, and Zack, Gary, and I spent the afternoon shooting baskets in Gary's driveway.

"Everyone want to go to the game tonight?" Zack asked.

"Definitely," Gary said.

"Wouldn't miss it," I said.

"Can't wait to see Julie again, can you?" Gary teased.

I just shrugged. "Jealous?"

"Not of you."

"Look, we all know that Brett's a very important part of Julie's life these days," Zack said with a smile, "but the Lewiston Eagles are a tough team and the Warriors have to win tonight *and* Monday night if we're gonna have any chance of making it to the county play-offs. I think Julie Valentine's going to be thinking a lot more about cheerleading than she is about Brett."

"Sounds okay with me," I said. "There's just one thing. I'm not waiting for you guys outside the gym. We're all going together."

"Brett needs protection from a girl." Gary couldn't resist needling me.

"I think it's Trey Boice he's worried about," said Zack.

*　*　*

I was in the bathroom after dinner, combing my hair, when someone knocked on the door.

"Who is it?" I asked.

"Nicole. Can I come in?"

"Do you have to?"

Instead of answering, she pushed open the bathroom door and came in. "You've been in here for almost twenty minutes."

"Don't you have anything better to do than time how long I'm in the bathroom?" I asked.

"Chill out, Brett," she said. "I just happened to notice. Usually you take about ten seconds to pull a comb through your hair. Got a big date?"

"Drop dead."

"Seriously."

"I'm going to the basketball game, okay?"

"Will Julie Valentine be there?"

"Maybe."

"Just maybe?"

"Okay, probably. I mean, she is the head cheerleader."

"So she'll definitely be there," Nicole said.

I put down the comb and glared at my sister. Sometimes she really got on my nerves. "Look, what is this?"

"I was only wondering why you were spending so much time combing your hair," Nicole said. "And now I have the answer."

"Well, you're wrong, okay? I didn't spend

twenty minutes combing my hair. I did other stuff, too." I checked my hair in the mirror one last time and then headed out.

"Make sure you give Julie a great big wet one for me!" Nicole yelled.

Sometimes I just wanted to kill her.

I put on my baseball cap and jacket and headed for Zack's house. We met at his front door. "Let's go," he said.

"Wait," I said. "Do me a favor, okay? Go back inside and get a hat and sunglasses."

"Why?"

"It's just a precaution."

Zack rolled his eyes like he thought I was nuts, but he went back inside and got a baseball cap and sunglasses.

From there we went to Gary's. I asked him to bring a hat and glasses, too.

"Are you serious?" he asked.

"He's serious," Zack said.

"What good is wearing sunglasses gonna do?" Gary asked.

"It's just in case I don't want to be seen," I said.

"Fine, so *you* wear them."

"Certain people know we're friends," I said.

"And you don't think that certain people may notice we're the only people in the gym wearing sunglasses and hats?"

"Maybe. Maybe not."

Gary shook his head wearily. "You're a certifiable head case, Brett."

"Just go back inside and get a hat and glasses, okay?"

"Sure."

We got to school early. The bleachers were still pretty empty.

"Great," Gary said, excitedly. "We can get courtside seats."

"I'd rather sit up there," I said, pointing to the seats at the top of the bleachers.

"Are you crazy?" Gary asked. "We never get seats like these."

"You can sit here if you like," I said. "But I'm going up there."

"What about you?" Gary asked Zack.

"It doesn't matter that much," Zack said. He and I started to climb up the bleachers.

Gary followed us, grumbling. "I can't believe I'm giving up the best seats in the gym because you're afraid you might be seen."

We climbed up to the very top row of the bleachers and sat down. I took off my jacket but kept my baseball cap on. Then I pulled out my sunglasses.

Out of the corner of my eye, I noticed Gary staring at me.

"Come on, guys," I said.

Gary sighed and put on his sunglasses. "This is

the dumbest thing I ever did. We probably look like the three blind mice sitting up here."

Pretty soon both teams came out and started taking warm-ups. More and more people were coming into the gym and the bleachers were filling up. A few people glanced at us in our sunglasses, but most didn't even notice.

The gym grew noisy and warm. Both teams finished their warm-ups and sat down on their benches for last-minute instructions from their coaches. Then the cheerleaders trotted out in single file, wearing their red-and-white outfits and carrying pom-poms. The crowd cheered.

Gary leaned toward me. "There she is, Romeo."

Julie was in the lead. She stared straight ahead and led the cheerleaders through a couple of cheers.

"I don't think she's going to notice you way up here," Zack said.

It looked like he was right. The ref blew his whistle and both teams headed for the court. Julie and the other cheerleaders finished their cheers. Julie glanced up once at the crowd, then sat down on the sidelines with the other cheerleaders to watch the game.

By halftime the game was tied and the gym was hot. Julie had acted pretty normal for a cheerleader — jumping around and shouting and trying to get the fans excited. During the game, each cheerleader was supposed to do a special cheer for one of the players. Julie did her cheer for Trey just before the half ended. When she finished, her cheeks were flushed and her pom-poms looked a little tattered.

"Looks like she's pretty into it," Gary said.

"She hasn't looked up here once," said Zack.

At halftime the players went into the locker rooms, and the cheerleaders did a halftime show.

"Know what?" Gary said.

"What?"

"I'm tired of wearing these sunglasses." He took his off.

"He's right," said Zack. "Julie and Trey have better things to do than worry about us."

I took off my sunglasses, too. A few minutes later, the players came out of the locker rooms and took warm-ups again. The cheerleaders headed for the sidelines. Just before she sat down Julie glanced up at the crowd. Her eyes went straight to mine.

"Uh-oh," Zack whispered.

Julie started to wave.

"What should I do?" I whispered.

"Wave back," Zack said.

I waved back. Julie smiled and nodded, then she sat down with the other cheerleaders.

Breeeeet! The ref blew his whistle and the second half began.

"See?" Gary said. "Nothing to worry about."

But no sooner were the words out of his mouth than Julie stood up and started to wave at me again.

10

Julie kept waving. The people sitting on the bleacher in front of her had to lean to the side to watch the game. Meanwhile, Julie was pointing at the floor beside her.

"What's she doing?" I whispered.

"I think she wants you to sit with her," Zack whispered back.

"What should I do?"

"Go sit with her." Gary grinned wickedly. "I'm sure Trey's too busy to notice."

"Drop dead."

"Put the glasses back on," Zack said.

I put on the glasses. Julie frowned a little and kept waving and gesturing for me to come down and sit with her.

"Hey, sit down!" someone in the bleachers shouted at her.

"Yeah, we're trying to watch the game!" yelled someone else.

Julie put her hands on her hips and glared at

them. Then she looked up at me with a sad expression on her face, but at least she sat down.

"Maybe we better leave," I whispered.

"No way!" Gary said. "This is a great game."

The game stayed close. When the third quarter ended, both teams headed for the bench with their backs to the crowd. The cheerleaders jumped up and started doing a cheer. Once again, Julie looked up at me and waved. Only this time she didn't wait until the end of the cheer to do it. She started waving right away. In fact, she wasn't even cheerleading. She just stood on the basketball court waving while the other girls danced and twirled around her.

In the crowd, heads began to turn as people looked to see who Julie was waving at.

"I think you're in trouble," Zack whispered.

"Get your sunglasses on!" I hissed. Zack and Gary put on their glasses, but more and more people kept turning to look at us.

Down on the sidelines, Jason Howard pointed to Julie and said something to Trey. I saw Trey's head begin to turn.

"Duck!" I dropped to my knees behind the people sitting in front of us. Zack and Gary did the same.

"Now what?" Gary whispered.

Zack peeked over the shoulders of the people sitting in front of us. "Look."

Gary and I looked up. Holding the basketball

under his arm, Trey had walked over to Julie and was talking to her. We couldn't hear what he was saying, but he looked pretty peeved. He kept pointing up at the bleachers. Everyone in the crowd was watching them. Julie stood with her arms crossed.

Trey finished talking and headed back to the bench, but as soon as he left, Julie stared up at the crowd and shaded her eyes with her hands. Trey got halfway back to the bench, then stopped and turned.

Thwamp! He slammed the basketball angrily to the ground and stormed back to her. He started shouting at her, but this time Julie ignored him. All of a sudden, Trey stopped shouting and stared up at the crowd, too.

Zack, Gary, and I quickly ducked down again.

"Emergency evacuation!" I whispered.

Still on my knees, I began to crawl along the bleacher. Gary and Zack followed. People had to pick their feet up to let us go by.

"Sorry!" I kept saying. "Ooops! Coming through! Sorry!"

Finally I got to the metal railing at the edge of the bleacher. If I went over the railing, it was about twenty-five feet straight down.

"We're trapped!" Gary groaned.

It looked bad. I peeked down at the basketball court. Julie was still searching the crowd with her eyes. Trey was standing next to her, doing the same thing.

I ducked back down.

"Got any ideas?" Zack asked.

"Just wait," I said.

Breeet! A moment later the ref blew his whistle and the fourth quarter began. Trey and his teammates headed back out to the court. Julie sat down.

"Okay, now!" I whispered, rising to a crouch and working my way down the side of the bleachers along the railing. When I got about two thirds of the way down, I quickly climbed over the railing and lowered myself to the floor on the other side.

Zack and Gary followed. A second later we ran out into the hall, grabbed our jackets, and dashed outside.

On the dark sidewalk outside the gym, Gary jumped in the air and raised a triumphant fist. "Ya-hoo!"

"We did it!" Zack shouted. They gave each other high fives.

"That was incredible!" Gary gasped.

"It was great!" Zack agreed.

"What are you guys talking about?" I asked.

They turned toward me with puzzled looks.

"That was an amazing escape," Gary said.

"From the *gym*?" I asked skeptically. "Who escapes from the gym? Besides, now we won't get to see the end of the game."

"What's bugging you?" Gary asked.

Before I could tell him, the gym door swung open and Julie rushed out, pulling on her jacket. I quickly grabbed Zack and Gary and ducked down behind some bushes.

"Brett?" she yelled. "Brett, where are you?"

She waited a moment. When no one answered, she ran toward the parking lot and disappeared into the dark.

Gary started to get up. "I don't believe it."

The gym door swung open again and Trey Boice rushed out in his basketball uniform, breathing hard. "Julie?" he shouted. "Julie, what's going on?"

Now Jason Howard and Adam Lampel rushed out. "Are you out of your mind, Trey?" Adam gasped. "You can't leave in the middle of the game."

"Coach Davis called a time-out," Jason said. "But you gotta get back in there before we blow it."

Trey didn't look happy.

"I don't know what's going on with Julie," he muttered angrily as they led him back inside. "But you better believe I'm gonna find out."

As soon as they'd gone, I jumped up. "Let's get out of here!" We started to run in the opposite direction from the way Julie had gone.

"That was totally bizarre." Zack puffed as he ran beside me in the dark. "Julie's acting like she doesn't care about anything except you."

"Is this some kind of joke?" Gary asked as he hurried behind us.

"If it is, no one's told me about it," I said.

"It doesn't look like they've told Trey either," Zack said.

Once we crossed the street that led to my neighborhood, we slowed down to a walk.

"Trey looked really mad." Gary's breath was coming out in white clouds.

"I don't think he's going to have a sense of humor about this," Zack said.

"What am I gonna do?" I asked.

"If I were you," Gary puffed, "I'd dig myself a grave so Trey won't have to get his hands dirty when he finds you on Monday morning."

"Stop trying to scare him," Zack said. "There's a good chance Trey still doesn't know who Brett is. I mean, what was the most he saw at the game? Three guys wearing baseball caps and sunglasses."

"Maybe," I said, "but if Julie keeps acting like this, it won't be long before he does figure out who I am."

"Look at it this way, Brett," Gary said. "You have all day tomorrow to come up with a plan."

"*Me?*" I asked. We stopped at my corner. "I thought it was *us*. I thought you said we were in this together."

"I've been thinking about that," Gary said. "You were right. Whatever's going on between you and Julie, it probably doesn't have anything to do with my dare. Besides, I have to go visit my grandparents tomorrow."

I looked at Zack.

"Sorry, *amigo*," Zack said. "I'm going to the boat show."

"So I guess you're on your own till Monday, bud," Gary said.

"Gee, thanks," I said.

"Hey," Zack patted me on the shoulder, "I have confidence in you. You'll think of something."

11

The next morning I wasn't thinking about much of anything when there was a knock on my bedroom door.

"Who is it?" I asked with a yawn.

"Your sister."

"Go away, I'm sleeping."

"I have something important for you," she said.

"Yeah, right."

"It's a letter."

"It's Sunday, meat brain. There's no mail."

"This didn't come by mail." Nicole pushed open the door. "It was hand-delivered."

She walked to my bed and waved a pink envelope at me. It gave off a familiar scent.

"Oh, no," I moaned.

"I even saw her," Nicole said.

"How?"

"I heard the mail slot bang and looked out the window just in time to see her drive away. Did you know she has a red sports car?"

"No."

"Well, she does." Nicole held up the envelope for me to see. On the front it said: *Mr. Brett Bergen.* On the back was a red lipstick mark.

"Sealed with a kiss." She winked.

"I don't believe this!" I groaned and pulled the covers over my head.

"Want me to read it?" Nicole said.

Normally I wouldn't let my sister touch my mail. But I was dreading what might be inside. "Go ahead."

"Goody." Nicole tore the letter open. For a few seconds I didn't hear anything.

"Well?"

"You won't believe this," Nicole warned.

"After last night I'll believe anything."

"What happened last night?"

"I'll tell you later. Now read."

"Okay. Ahem." Nicole cleared her throat. " 'Dearest Brett . . .' "

"Are you making this up?" I interrupted.

"You want to see it for yourself?" Nicole asked.

"No, go ahead. I believe you."

"All right. 'Dearest Brett, I saw you at the game last night. I hope I didn't embarrass you in front of your friends. If I did, please accept my apology. I'm writing this note because it seems so hard for us to find time to get together at school. I wish we could spend some time together. You seem like such an interesting and fascinating person . . .' "

Nicole paused.

"What's wrong?" I asked.

"She must be talking about someone else. Is there anyone else at school named Brett Bergen?"

"I wish. What else does it say?"

"Let's see." Nicole started to read again. " 'After those few moments we shared at the dance Friday night, I could tell we have a lot in common. Please call me. I've enclosed my phone number. It's too bad I promised you-know-who I'd go shopping with him today. But I should be home after four o'clock, and I really hope you'll call.' "

"That's it?" I said.

"She signed it with a lot of X's and O's."

"What's that mean?" I pulled the blanket off my head.

"You don't know?" Nicole looked surprised.

"Give me a break, Miss Know-It-All."

"Well, it sort of means love and kisses," Nicole said.

"Great!" I hid my face in my hands.

"Is this you-know-who Mr. Three-Letter All-County everything?" Nicole asked.

"You got it."

"So what happened last night?"

I told her.

"Guess I owe you an apology," Nicole said.

"What for?"

"Remember I said you had an overinflated ego?"

"Yes."

"It looks like I was wrong. As incredible as it may seem, the girl from the Miller's department store ads really likes you."

"What should I do?" I asked.

"Well, do you like her?" Nicole asked.

"This has nothing to do with whether I like her or not," I said. "She's a senior. She's the most popular, beautiful girl in the school, and she's Trey Boice's girlfriend."

"Doesn't matter," Nicole said. "The power of love can overcome any obstacle."

"You wouldn't say that if you saw Trey Boice."

I hung around the house all day. Normally I might have gone to the mall and hung out there, but with my luck I would have run into Julie and Trey.

I was watching an afternoon basketball game on TV when Nicole came into the den.

"It's just after four o'clock," she said.

"So?"

"Julie's waiting for your call."

"There's not going to be any call," I said.

"She'll be disappointed."

"Get lost."

Nicole was just turning to leave when the den phone rang.

"I'll get it," she said.

Suddenly I had a thought. "Wait!"

Nicole stopped. "What?"

"If it's Julie, I'm not here."

Nicole picked up the phone. "Hello? . . . Oh, uh, he's not here. . . . Well, I'm not sure when he'll be back. . . . I don't really know where he went. . . . Oh, no. Nothing like that. . . . Sure, okay, I'll tell him you called."

Nicole hung up. "Guess who?"

"Unbelievable." I shook my head wearily.

"She really likes you," Nicole said. "I could hear it in her voice."

I nodded sadly. "I didn't get the part where you said, 'Nothing like that.' What was that about?"

"She wanted to know if you were out with your girlfriend."

"What girlfriend?" I asked.

"Oh, come on, Brett, don't be so thick," Nicole said. "That's the oldest trick in the book. She was just trying to find out if you have one, that's all."

"Then you should have told her I *was* out with my girlfriend," I said. "Maybe she'd get the message."

"Can I be blunt?" Nicole asked.

"Sure."

"I don't think it would have made a bit of difference."

*　　*　　*

The phone rang every fifteen minutes for the rest of the afternoon. Mom and Dad went out with friends for dinner, and ordered a pizza for us. But Nicole and I couldn't eat in peace.

"No, I'm sorry, but he's *still* not home," Nicole said into the kitchen phone. "Yes, I *promise* I'll tell him to call you as soon as he gets in."

She hung up and gave me an exasperated look. "She's really getting to be a pain."

"I know."

My sister sat down and picked up her half-eaten slice of pizza with mushrooms and sausage. "Maybe you better talk to her next time she calls."

The thought filled me with dread. "Just help me through this tonight and I promise you can pick all the TV shows for the next month."

"That's not the point, Brett. Sooner or later she's going to figure out that you're here and just not answering the phone."

"The next time she calls, tell her I'm sleeping over at a friend's house."

"She'll ask for your friend's number."

"Say it's unlisted," I said. "Tell her my friend's father is a doctor and you've sworn you won't give the number out."

"She won't buy it, Brett."

"Just try, okay?"

Nicole rolled her eyes. "You're going to owe me for this. And I mean, big time."

The minutes ticked by. Usually I could put away two or three slices of pizza at dinner without any trouble. But that night I hardly finished one. My stomach felt tight and I didn't have much of an appetite.

Ding-dong!

Something rang, but it wasn't the phone.

"The doorbell," Nicole said. She and I looked at each other. "You don't think . . ."

I nodded miserably. "Anything's possible."

Nicole pulled back the shade on the kitchen window and peeked out. "Her car's in the driveway."

"Great," I groaned. "What do we do now?"

"I love that car," Nicole said. "Couldn't we all go for a ride?"

"No!"

Nicole made a face. "You're no fun."

"Thanks for the compliment," I said. "Now please answer the door and tell her I'm not here."

"Only if I get to pick all the TV shows for the next *two* months," Nicole said.

"Okay, fine." At that point I was willing to agree with anything.

"Hide in the den and turn off the lights," Nicole said.

I followed her instructions, but I couldn't resist opening the den door just a hair and peeking out. Meanwhile, Nicole opened the front door. Julie was standing there, wearing a short ski parka and jeans.

"Oh, hi," she said. "I just happened to be driving by."

Driving by? I thought. *Our street runs into a dead end!*

"Brett didn't come in, did he?" Julie asked.

"Nope," Nicole said. "He's still out."

"You must be his little sister," Julie said. "How old are you?"

"Ten," Nicole said. "I'm two years younger than Brett, who happens to be twelve, you know."

Julie smiled knowingly. "He's very mature for his age."

"Oh, really?" Nicole said. "I hadn't noticed."

"Well, you're his sister."

"I pride myself on being extremely objective," said Nicole.

Julie was unfazed. "You still have no idea when he'll be back?"

"None," Nicole said. "Sometimes he stays out all night."

"But there's school tomorrow. He has to sleep."

"He catches up in class."

Julie looked at her watch. "Well, all right. But please make sure he calls me. Even if he gets home late."

"I will." Nicole started to close the door, but Julie paused in the doorway and looked around as if she didn't want to leave.

"Bye-bye." Nicole pushed the door closed.

I let myself out of the den.

"Sooner or later you're going to have to face her," Nicole said.

"And what about Trey Boice?" I asked.

Rap! Rap! Before Nicole could answer my question, there was a sharp knock on the door. Nicole's eyes went wide and she quickly waved me back into the den. I pulled the door closed until there was just a hair-sized crack to watch through.

Nicole pulled open the door, and brought her hand to her mouth. I guess we'd both expected Julie Valentine to be there.

But we were wrong.

Standing in the doorway was Trey Boice.

And he looked mad.

12

W here is he?" Trey said, stepping past Nicole into the living room.

"Who?"

"Your older brother."

Nicole swallowed nervously. "Uh, what older brother?"

"The older brother Julie just came to see," Trey said, looking around. "The older brother she's been trying to call for the last two hours. The older brother who wants to steal her away from me."

"There's no older brother like that here," Nicole said.

"Don't give me that," Trey fumed. He went over to the kitchen doorway and looked in. "I know he's here. I followed Julie. He's hiding, right?"

"No, really, there's nobody like that here."

"Gimme a break," Trey said. "There's two plates on the kitchen table."

Trey backed out of the kitchen doorway and went down the hall. He pushed open the door to the closet. "He's here, and when I find him he's gonna be real sorry."

"Listen, uh, sir," said Nicole, "I don't know who you are, but — "

"I'm Trey Boice," Trey said. "Julie Valentine is *my* girlfriend. And I intend to keep it that way."

He turned and stared at the den door. Inside I quickly backed away. My heart was pounding with fear. What was I gonna do? Where was I gonna hide?

The couch! I got on my stomach and slid under it. The carpet was really dusty.

"Please don't go in there," I heard Nicole beg. But it was too late. From my vantage point under the couch I saw the den door swing open. The den light flashed on and a large pair of slightly dirty Nike basketball sneakers stepped in.

"There's no one in there," Nicole gasped. "I swear."

The dust was itching my nose. I was gonna sneeze! I tried to stop it, but it was no use. "Ha-choo!"

"Oh yeah?" Trey said. The sneakers stepped toward the couch. Two denim-covered knees touched the carpet, followed by two hands. Then Trey Boice's face appeared.

"Who're you, kid?" Trey asked.

"Uh, nobody."

"What are you doing under here?"

"Nothing."

Trey frowned. "Where is he?"

"Who?" I asked.

"Your older brother."

"I don't have an older brother."

"Oh, yeah? Then who does Julie keep calling? Who'd she just come here to see?"

"Oh, uh, *that* older brother," I said, thinking fast. "I think he just went out."

"Don't give me that. I followed Julie here. I didn't see her leave with anyone."

"He went out the back," I said.

Trey blinked. "I'll bet he's meeting Julie somewhere! Where'd he say he was going?"

"He didn't."

"Darn!" Trey jumped to his feet and I watched his basketball sneakers retreat from the den.

"I'm gonna go find that guy," Trey shouted as he stormed back out through the living room. "But if he gets back here first, you give him a message, okay? You tell him that if he ever goes near Julie again he's a dead man. You got that? *He's dog food!*"

Wham! The front door slammed shut. Under the couch I breathed a deep sigh . . . and got another noseful of dust.

"Ha-choo!"

A small pair of feet in white socks came toward

the couch. Nicole got on her hands and knees and looked at me.

"Quick thinking," she said.

"Thanks." I started to crawl out.

"He thinks it must be someone older."

"For now," I said woefully.

13

You look really tired," Nicole said the next morning at breakfast.

"I didn't sleep well." I yawned. "I kept having this nightmare about being trapped in a small cage with a large man-eating dog."

"Worried about going to school today?"

"What do *you* think?"

"Maybe it won't be so bad," Nicole said.

"Oh, sure. I can just see Julie swooping down on me in the school hallway with Trey right behind."

"When he finds out it's you, maybe he'll think it's a big joke."

"Or maybe he'll just feed me to Killer."

"Well, I have one good piece of news," Nicole said.

"What's that?"

"School starts in twenty minutes so you won't have to wait long to find out."

We rinsed our dishes and put them in the dishwasher, then headed for school. It was cold and clear outside and we hadn't gotten very far down the sidewalk when a red sports car pulled up to the curb.

"I guess you're not going to have to wait until school to see Julie," Nicole said.

Julie rolled down the window and waved. "Hi, Nicole." She gave me a big smile. "Hi, Brett."

"Hi." I quickly looked around, but there was no sign of Trey. Still, I thought it was a good idea to keep walking.

The red sports car rolled along on the street beside us. I kept my eyes straight ahead. But Nicole was looking at the car.

"Nice wheels," she said.

"Thanks," replied Julie. "Need a ride to school?"

Nicole looked up at me with pleading eyes. "Please, Brett."

I shook my head. "Thanks, Julie, but we'd prefer to walk."

"Says who?" Nicole crossed her arms and pouted.

"Don't do this to me," I whispered.

"What's the big deal?" Nicole whispered back. "Either way you have to go to school."

"Yeah, but not with *her*."

"Well, I'm going." Nicole stepped off the sidewalk toward the sports car.

"Oh, all right," I said. I followed her and got in.

"I guess you're going to the elementary school first," Julie said as she put the car in gear and took off.

"Yup," Nicole said, staring at the dashboard. "So how long have you had this baby?"

"Almost a year," Julie said. "My parents got it for me when I made National Honor Society."

"Cool."

Julie glanced at me and winked. A few moments later she pulled up in front of the elementary school.

"Can't we go around the block a couple of times?" Nicole asked.

"Maybe another time," Julie said. "Right now, Brett and I have to get to school."

"Darn." Nicole got out. "Anyway, thanks for the ride."

"Anytime." Julie put the car in gear again and accelerated.

"Cute kid," she said.

"Once in a while," I replied.

Julie turned to me and smiled warmly. "So, finally, we're alone."

"Yes."

"Are you nervous?"

"Yes."

Julie grinned. "Me, too, a little."

"Uh, I hope you don't mind me saying this," I said. "But this doesn't make any sense."

"Feelings don't have to make sense, Brett."

"Well, maybe that's true," I said. "But you're a beautiful senior model and I'm a seventh-grader. If people see us together, they're gonna think it's weird."

"Why are you so worried about what people think?" Julie asked.

"Mostly because one of them is Trey Boice."

Julie chuckled. "Don't worry, he's a teddy bear."

"He may be a teddy bear, but I hear Killer's not exactly a lamb chop."

Julie pulled into the student's parking lot. I was getting out of the car when I saw Trey coming toward us. He didn't look happy.

"Uh-oh." I started to back away.

Trey walked right past me like I wasn't there. "I think we better talk," he told Julie.

"Not now," Julie said.

"Yes, right now," Trey insisted.

"No," Julie said, sliding her arm through mine. "Not in front of Brett."

Trey frowned. "Who?"

"Brett."

Trey looked down and squinted at me. "Haven't I seen you somewhere before?"

"Last night," I said. "Under the couch."

"The couch . . ." Trey muttered. His eyes suddenly bulged as he realized what that meant. He looked at Julie and then back at me.

"It's *you*?" he sputtered.

"Don't act so surprised," Julie said.

"What are you talking about?" Trey shouted excitedly. "Are you out of your mind? He's a kid. He's nothing."

"That's funny," Julie replied calmly. "To me, he's everything. Come on, Brett, let's go." The next thing I knew, we started to walk arm in arm toward the school entrance.

Inside school, kids were at their lockers, hanging up their coats and dumping their books. As Julie and I came down the hall, every single one of them stopped what they were doing and stared at us.

Finally, we got to my locker. Gary and Zack were already at theirs. As I undid my lock, Julie leaned against the wall and gave me that dreamy gaze. The flowers I'd tried to give her on Valentine's Day were still lying on the top shelf of my locker, looking pretty wilted. I glanced at them and sighed as I hung up my jacket.

"I guess we won't get to see each other until lunch," Julie said, kind of sadly.

"Yeah," I replied. *If I live that long.*

"I'll be thinking of you every minute," Julie said. "I hope you'll be thinking of me."

"Oh, yeah," I said. I'd be thinking of Julie, and Trey, *and Killer* . . .

Julie blew me a kiss and walked away down the hall.

Everyone watched her go, then turned and

stared at me in awe. Gary and Zack closed their lockers and came over.

"That was the most amazing thing I ever saw," Zack said.

"Oh, Brett," Gary said breathlessly, "I'll be thinking of you, too."

"This never would have happened if it wasn't for you," I said angrily.

Gary looked surprised. "You really think it's my fault that Julie Valentine fell in love with you?"

"Listen, Gary." Zack nudged him. "Next time get her to fall in love with me, okay?"

They both grinned.

"It's not funny," I said. "Trey knows who I am. I'll be lucky if I'm still in one piece by the end of the day."

"Hey, what can I tell you?" Gary said with a shrug. "All's fair in love and war."

14

I didn't see Julie or Trey all morning. At lunch-time I went to my locker to get my lunch, then I walked over to Gary's locker. Gary was bent over, trying to find something.

"Going to lunch?" I asked.

"Yeah, but Zack wants me to help him carry an enlarger to the darkroom first," he said. "You can go ahead. We'll meet you."

"No way."

Gary looked up from his locker. "What's the problem now?"

"Julie's gonna be there," I said.

"She'll be on the other side of the cafeteria," Zack said, joining us.

"Don't bet on it," I said.

Gary straightened up and slammed his locker closed. "Listen, Brett, I don't care what's going on between you two. In the history of Snorkwaller High no senior has ever eaten lunch on our side of the cafeteria."

"No senior who looked like Julie Valentine ever had a crush on a seventh-grader either," I reminded him.

"It's dumb to argue about this," Zack said. "We'll all go to the darkroom. Then we can all go to the cafeteria together and protect Brett from his girlfriend."

I helped them carry the enlarger to the darkroom, and then we went down to the cafeteria.

"No matter what happens when we get there," I said nervously, "I expect you guys to stick with me."

"I'm telling you, Brett," Gary said. "There's no way Julie's gonna come over and sit on the junior high side."

We stepped into the cafeteria and froze in our footsteps.

"You're right," I said with a gulp.

Julie wasn't waiting for us at our table.

Trey Boice was.

"I think I just lost my appetite," Gary muttered.

"Me, too," said Zack.

"Me, three," I agreed.

We started to back up toward the exit. Suddenly we bumped into something. Turning around, we found Adam Lampel and Jason Howard blocking our escape route.

"You weren't leaving, were you?" Adam asked.

"Yeah, you little geeks just got here," said Jason.

Adam and Jason shoved us toward Trey.

"Have a seat, Brett," Trey said, pointing across the table.

"Uh, what about my friends?" I asked nervously.

Trey shrugged like he didn't care. Gary, Zack, and I sat down. I quickly scanned the cafeteria.

"Don't bother looking for Julie," Trey said. "She's got a cheerleading meeting." He leaned across the table and glowered at me. "I got a big problem, Brett. Know what it is?"

"Uh, Julie?"

"Julie's only part of it. Know what the rest of my problem is?"

I shook my head.

"Look around the cafeteria."

I looked around. From one end of the cafeteria to the other, it seemed like everyone had stopped what they were doing and were staring at us. Even the janitor, Mr. Grooms, was standing there with his mop and bucket.

"Want to know what the biggest joke going around school is?" Trey asked.

It seemed like an odd time for him to want to tell a joke, but I wasn't going to argue. "Uh, okay."

"Me," Trey said. "Because everybody knows some geek seventh-grader stole my girl."

"That's not true," I gasped. "I didn't steal her."

"Oh, yeah?" Trey raised an eyebrow. "Did you read that article she wrote in the paper?"

"Sort of."

"Did you ask her to be your valentine?"

"Yeah, but I never thought . . ."

"Never thought what?"

"Uh, that she'd take me seriously."

"That makes two of us." Trey leaned back and studied me for a moment. "But guess what?"

I swallowed. "She did."

Trey nodded. It got very quiet. There was an ominous look in Trey's eyes. He made a fist and cracked his knuckles. "Know what I have to do now?"

"No."

"I have to make you pay."

A chill ran down my spine. "Do you really think that's necessary? I mean, considering the fact that I never really meant any harm?"

"Doesn't matter," Trey replied. "See, it's a matter of appearances, Brett. If you don't pay, I look like the biggest dork who ever attended Snorkwaller High."

"But that's impossible," I said. "You're the captain of the basketball team. You're a three-letter man. You're — "

" — the guy whose girl was stolen by a seventh-grader," Trey finished the sentence for me. He started to get up. "Come on, Brett, let's go outside and get it over with."

I stared out the window of the cafeteria. It was a dull, cold gray day and I could easily picture my twisted corpse lying on the frozen brown ground.

"Uh, I better not," I said. "It looks awful cold outside and I didn't bring my jacket."

Bang! Trey slammed his hands on the table and leaned toward me. "Look," he growled, "if you want me to do it in here, I will. But I'd hate to make a mess in the cafeteria."

Out of the corner of my eye I saw Mr. Grooms nod in agreement. I looked around quickly, searching for a teacher who might save me.

"Forget it, Brett," Trey said. "Even if you manage to get out of it now, I'll wait for you after school. I know where you live. You can't escape, so you might as well be a man and get it over with."

"Actually, I'd still rather wait until after school," I said.

"Hey, Trey," said Adam Lampel. "Didn't you say you forgot to feed Killer this morning?"

Trey grinned. "That's right, Brett. If you wait till after school, I might have to feed you to Killer."

"I think I just changed my mind," I said, starting to get up. Everyone was watching me. Some people looked sympathetic, others had mean smiles on their faces as if I deserved to be slaughtered.

"Uh, excuse me a second." It was Zack.

Trey stared at him. "What?"

"My name is Zack Warner and I'm a friend of Brett's."

"So?"

"I was wondering if you could hold off beating up Brett for just twenty-four hours," Zack said.

"Why?" Trey asked.

"Well, let's be honest," Zack said. "You don't really want to beat up Brett. What you really want is to get Julie to come back to you. Now, the thing is, Julie hasn't really spent much time with Brett. I, on the other hand, have known Brett for most of my life, and I am confident that once Julie gets to know him, she'll go back to you."

"Gee, thanks," I grumbled.

"Hey, I'm just being honest," Zack said.

"Well, maybe I really do want to beat up Brett," Trey said. "And maybe I really don't want Julie to get to know Brett any better than she already does."

"Hmmm . . ." Zack rubbed his chin. "All right, then how about this? Suppose Brett promises you he'll stay away from her for the next twenty-four hours?"

"What's the point?" Trey asked.

"The point is . . ." Zack thought fast. "You have

an important basketball game tonight. Do you really want to risk injuring your hands by beating up Brett before the game?"

Trey frowned. It was obvious he hadn't considered this. "You're right. Okay. He gets twenty-four hours, but only if he swears he won't go near Julie."

Zack nudged me hard in the ribs.

"I swear," I yelped.

Trey and his buddies got up and left. I sank back down to the lunch table and pressed my fingers against my temples.

"Tah-dah!" Zack grinned proudly.

I rolled my eyes and shook my head.

"Hey," Gary said. "Can't you show some appreciation for what Zack did?"

"What did he do?" I asked.

"He saved your life," Gary said.

"Great," I moped. "So all I have to look forward to for the next twenty-four hours is getting beaten into a pulp or fed to a hungry German shepherd."

"But now you have options," Zack said.

I looked up at him. "Like what?"

"Well . . ." Zack thought for a moment. "You can stay home sick for the rest of the year. Or you could quickly enroll in private school. The least you could do is go out this afternoon and buy a life insurance policy naming me as your beneficiary."

"Thanks a lot," I moaned.

"Come on, I was only trying to do you a favor," Zack said, a little hurt.

"Yeah, I know," I said, feeling bad for him. "It's just that what I really need right now is a miracle."

15

I managed to avoid Julie for the rest of the day. After school I picked up Nicole and walked her home.

"For a guy who's got the most beautiful girlfriend in school, you look pretty bummed out," she said.

"Maybe it's because in approximately twenty hours and forty-six minutes her former boyfriend is going to break every bone in my body."

"Really?"

I nodded miserably.

"Do you think I could have your mountain bike?" Nicole asked. "The gears don't work on mine."

"Thanks, Nicole," I said. "It's nice to know you have my best interests at heart."

"So what are you going to do?" she asked.

"I don't know. What would *you* do?"

"Take an intensive course in self-defense?"

I shook my head. "Not enough time."

"You could go to Trey's house, get on your hands and knees, and beg for mercy."

"Forget it. I'm not going near his house. Besides, I don't think Trey's the merciful type."

"Hmmm." Nicole thought for a moment. "Okay, want to know what I'd really do?"

"Yes."

"I'd try to figure out how this happened," she said. "I mean, no offense, Brett, but asking a girl like Julie to be your valentine usually doesn't make her fall head over heels in love with you."

"Even if she really believes in the romance of Valentine's Day?"

"Even then," Nicole said.

"So what should I do?" I asked.

"Try to remember what happened that made her fall in love with you."

"That's easy. Gary, Zack, and I agreed that whoever missed sinking his lunch bag in the garbage would have to ask Julie to be his valentine. And since I lost, I asked her."

"There has to be more to it," Nicole said. Ahead of us was the gate to E. N. Chanter's mansion.

"Well, I tried to give her those flowers from Mr. Chanter's greenhouse, but she pricked her finger on the thorn."

"Interesting," Nicole mused. "Like Sleeping Beauty."

"Only she didn't fall asleep," I said. "I mean, now I kind of wish she had."

Suddenly Nicole stopped. "That's it!" she gasped. "She didn't fall asleep, she fell in love!"

"What are you talking about?" I asked.

"There must have been something about those flowers that made Julie Valentine fall in love with you."

"Are you cra — " I started to say, then remembered something. "Wait a minute! Remember that day we snuck into the greenhouse? You took a big sniff of that purple flower and then you hugged me and said I was your hero."

Nicole shook her head. "You're the one who's crazy."

"No. Believe me, Nicole, you did."

"No way," Nicole said. "But even if it was true, so what?"

"That was the same flower Julie pricked her finger on," I said.

Beep! Beep! I heard a car horn and turned to see a red sports car coming down the street.

"Quick!" I grabbed Nicole by the arm and we started to run. We turned the corner and I pulled her inside the big iron gate in front of Mr. Chanter's driveway. We hid behind the tall brick wall beside the gate.

"What's going on?" Nicole asked.

"I don't want her to see us," I said. "Besides, I promised Trey I wouldn't go near her for twenty-four hours."

Out on the street we heard the car turn the

corner and stop. A car door opened and Julie called my name. "Brett? Oh, Brett, darling, where are you?"

"Brett, *darling*?" Nicole whispered in disbelief.

"*Shhhhhh.* I don't want her to find us," I whispered back.

"Brett?" Julie called. "Oh, please don't hide. I must see you. I *have* to see you. I missed you today."

"She sounds a little desperate," Nicole whispered.

I nodded. Julie did sound desperate. *Desperately in love.* She called my name a few more times, and then we finally heard the car door close and the car drive away.

"I think she's gone," Nicole said.

"Boy, I don't know what's worse," I said. "Trey Boice wanting to kill me, or Julie Valentine being madly in love with me."

"Is that a problem?" a voice asked.

Nicole and I jumped around. Standing behind us was E. N. Chanter.

16

His long white hair fell to his shoulders and his face looked old and creased. He was wearing gardening gloves, and carried an empty flowerpot in one hand and a trowel in the other. Neither Nicole nor I knew what to say.

"Who have we here?" he asked. "The neighbor children, I believe. Haven't I seen your faces gazing down at me from your upstairs windows? Yes, I believe I have. Welcome to the neighborhood. If you ever need anything, don't ask me for it."

"Are you E. N. Chanter?" I asked.

"It would be difficult not to be," he replied.

Nicole and I gave each other a look. He sure had an odd way of speaking.

"What does the E stand for?" Nicole asked.

"The E?" Mr. Chanter scratched his head. "Everything, I suppose."

"Then what does the N stand for?" my sister asked.

"The N? Why, Nothing, of course."

This guy is definitely weird, I thought.

"We have to ask you a really important question," Nicole said.

"Do I have to give an important answer?" Mr. Chanter asked.

Nicole and I glanced worriedly at each other.

"Do you think it's possible for someone to prick their finger on a certain flower stem and fall madly in love?" Nicole asked.

Mr. Chanter's snow-white eyebrows rose in surprise. "So you're the ones who took my flowers."

"Not me," Nicole said. "Him."

Mr. Chanter squinted at me. His eyes were sort of greenish. "Little did you know what you were getting yourself into."

"How'd you know they were missing?" I asked. "I mean, you must have a million flowers in that greenhouse."

"I know every one of them," Mr. Chanter said. "So you pricked your finger and fell hopelessly in love with someone?"

"No, someone pricked their finger and fell hopelessly in love with me," I said.

"Then what's the problem?"

"It was the wrong person," I said. "And now her boyfriend wants to feed me to his dog."

Mr. Chanter nodded. "Serves you right for taking what isn't yours."

"But I'm really sorry," I said desperately. "I swear I'll never do it again. Can't you help?"

Mr. Chanter studied me. "How old are you, son?"

"Twelve."

"I don't suppose people marry that young anymore, do they?"

"Are you serious?" I said. "No way."

"And may I assume that you wouldn't be willing to make an exception?" he asked.

"I couldn't," I stammered. "I mean, it's impossible. It's probably not even legal."

"Hmm, yes, laws," Mr. Chanter mumbled. "They do have a way of interfering with things, don't they?"

"Why did you ask if Brett would get married?" Nicole asked.

"Because the flower his lady friend pricked her finger on was from the rare Amazonian Passion plant," Mr. Chanter explained. "I discovered it myself in the rain forests of Brazil only a few years ago. Mine is the only one in captivity. A mere whiff of its fragrance is enough to cause serious attraction. A deeper sniff will create an hour or two of sublime infatuation."

"And if someone pricks their finger on a thorn?" Nicole asked.

Mr. Chanter looked very solemn. "They will fall hopelessly in love with the first person they see."

Nicole turned to me. "Nice going, Brett."

"You mean, like, *forever*?" I asked in disbelief.

Mr. Chanter nodded. "Once it's in the bloodstream, it's there to stay."

"What am I going to do?" I asked.

"You're going to get off my property before I call the police and have you charged with burglary," Mr. Chanter said abruptly, and started to walk away.

"Wait!" I shouted. "You're probably the only person in the world who can help me."

"That's true," Mr. Chanter said with his back to me.

"Why won't you?"

"Why should I?" he asked, still walking away. "All you've done is steal from me."

"Well, I'll . . . I'll make it up to you somehow," I shouted.

Mr. Chanter stopped and turned. "And how would you propose to do that?"

"Uh, my dad and mom own a glass company," I said. "Maybe I could get them to fix some of your windows."

"*Maybe* did you say?" Mr. Chanter asked. "What kind of promise is that? I'm supposed to help you out of this terrible mess and all you can promise me is that *maybe* you'll fix my windows?"

"Okay, okay," I said desperately. "I *promise* they'll fix some of your windows."

"*Double* promise?" Mr. Chanter asked.

"Yes," I said.

"Only *some* of the windows?"

I glanced up at the house. There were broken and cracked windows everywhere. And I remembered the greenhouse was in pretty bad shape, too. "Gee, Mr. Chanter, that's a lot of windows."

"You're right." Mr. Chanter started to walk away again. "Enjoy being eaten. I hear that only the first dozen or so bites really hurt."

"Okay!" I shouted again. "I double promise you'll have *all* your windows fixed."

Mr. Chanter stopped and smiled.

"Mom and Dad are gonna kill you," Nicole whispered.

"They may kill me," I whispered back. "But at least they won't eat me."

17

As Mr. Chanter led us up the long, winding driveway he told us about his profession.

"I'm an olfactologist," he said. "I study the effect certain smells have on the brain."

"What kind of effect?" I asked.

"All kinds," he said. "For instance. Have you ever smelled something and it reminded you of a place you'd once been?"

"Oh, sure," Nicole said. "Every time my mom melts chocolate for baking I think of when we visited the Hershey chocolate factory."

"And every time I smell cigar smoke I think of grandpa," I said. "Because he always smokes cigars."

"Precisely," said Mr. Chanter. "Smells have the power to evoke memories. They can also make us feel certain emotions. Take perfume, for instance. In fact, I used to be a perfumer."

"What's that?" Nicole asked.

"I made perfumes," Mr. Chanter explained. "I

was obsessed with finding the perfect combination of floral oils and extracts that would make even the most horrible person glow with emotion."

"Did you find it?" I asked as he led us to his greenhouse and opened the door.

"No . . . and yes." Mr. Chanter held open the door and Nicole and I went inside. "I discovered that it was impossible to make the perfect perfume because the perfect ingredients had not been found. So I set out to find them."

"And that's what these plants are?" Nicole guessed.

"In some cases, yes. In some cases, almost." Mr. Chanter swept his arm around, taking in the entire greenhouse. "Many of these plants are mutations and crossbreeds, genetically engineered to yield the perfect ingredients for the perfect perfume."

He started to walk through the greenhouse. Nicole and I followed.

"So have you made the perfect perfume?" Nicole asked.

"Have I?" Mr. Chanter accidentally brushed against a plant with thick green leaves and large orange flowers. "Have I? Ha-ha! *Ha-hah-haah!*"

He began to laugh like a madman. It was the same loud laughter we'd heard coming from the greenhouse ever since we'd moved in next door. Nicole and I gave each other nervous looks.

"Ah-ha-hah!" Mr. Chanter laughed and pointed

at the plant he'd just brushed against. "Watch out for that one. Hee-hee. It causes uncontrollable laughter. I keep forgetting to prune it back. Har-har."

Nicole and I steered clear of the laughing plant. Soon Mr. Chanter had calmed down to a few giggles.

"Where was I?" he asked.

"I asked if you've made the perfect perfume?" Nicole said.

"No." Mr. Chanter shook his head. "Because I realized that to do so would be irresponsible. We simply couldn't have everyone falling in love with everyone else, now could we?"

"But that's just what's happened," I said. "I mean, between Julie Valentine and me."

"Ah, yes." Mr. Chanter stopped beside the plant with the deep purple flowers. Then he turned his gaze on me. "I suppose you want me to come up with some sort of antidote that will stop this young woman from being madly in love with you."

"Yes, please. If you can."

Mr. Chanter rubbed his chin. "Well, I can probably do it, but it will take a few weeks."

"It can't!" I gasped.

"Why not?" Mr. Chanter asked.

"I've only got until tomorrow at lunch. Then I either get beaten to a pulp or turned into dog food."

Mr. Chanter nodded pensively. "You know, I've noticed you take care of your lawn. One thing I've always wanted was a nice, well-kept green lawn."

"But what about fixing the windows?" I asked.

"The windows are for my agreeing to make the antidote," Mr. Chanter said. "The lawn would be for making it *tonight*."

"So what would I have to do?" I asked, feeling dismal.

"Oh, not that much. Just get rid of all those weeds and shrubs, then turn over all the soil, then seed."

"Uh, how much property do you have?" I asked.

"Just over three acres."

I felt really ill. But what choice did I have? "Okay, Mr. Chanter, you drive a hard bargain, but if you make the antidote, I'll do it."

"Very good," Mr. Chanter said. "Stop by on the way to school tomorrow morning."

"Thanks, Mr. Chanter, really."

"Remember, you'll not only have to put the lawn in, but mow it as well. And don't forget, I expect *all* the windows to be fixed."

"I know, Mr. Chanter. Believe me, I know."

18

That afternoon, the phone rang every half hour as Julie called, looking for me. After dinner she stopped by, but Nicole told her I was in bed with a bad case of the flu. Julie wanted to hang around anyway, but my sister reminded her that there was another basketball game that night and she was expected to cheerlead.

The next morning I was in my room getting dressed when there was a knock on the door.

"Who is it?" I asked.

"Nicole. Guess who's waiting for you in the kitchen?"

"Oh, no! How'd she get in?"

"She came to the front door with some chicken soup she said would make you feel better. Then she wanted to put it in the refrigerator. Now she says she just wants to come up and see how you're feeling."

"Give me five minutes," I said. "Then let her

up. I won't be here. Meet me over at Mr. Chanter's house."

Nicole went downstairs. I put on a heavy sweater, opened my bedroom window, and climbed down one of the drainpipes from the roof gutters.

I was sneaking across our backyard when I heard Julie shout, "Brett, wait!"

I turned and saw her sliding open the kitchen door. She must have seen me from inside. Now she was running across the yard toward me.

I took off for the wall.

"Please, Brett, wait!" she cried.

I made it to the ladder and quickly climbed up. Then I pulled the ladder up so Julie couldn't follow. She ran to the wall and looked up at me.

"You don't have the flu," she said.

"I did. I made a miraculous recovery."

"No, you didn't. You just don't like me." Her eyes started to fill with tears.

"Julie, it's not that I don't like you," I said. "It's just that we're wrong for each other. You're a senior and I'm in seventh grade. I mean, I know love is sometimes blind, but this is ridiculous."

"I don't care what anyone says," Julie sobbed. "I'll love you forever."

School was going to start soon. I was running out of time. "I really have to go. I'll see you in school, okay?"

"You promise you won't avoid me?" Julie asked, wiping her eyes.

"I promise."

"Can't I give you a ride?"

"Not today," I said.

Julie nodded sadly and started to walk away. I quickly climbed down the tree into Mr. Chanter's yard.

"Brett!" Nicole called as she came around the side of Mr. Chanter's house. "What happened with Julie?"

"I promised her I'd see her at school." I pushed open the door to the greenhouse. "Let's see what Mr. Chanter came up with."

We found Mr. Chanter sitting at a wooden table inside the greenhouse. The table was covered with leather-bound books, piles of dried leaves, vials of liquid, and plastic bags.

"Ah, Brett, Nicole," he said. "I've been waiting for you."

"Good news?" I asked hopefully.

"Well, some good and some bad."

"What's the bad news?" Nicole asked.

"I haven't been able to find an antidote."

I felt my heart sink. "Then what's the good news?"

Mr. Chanter held up a small plastic bag with two dark leaves inside. "These leaves, when burned, will allow the young lady to switch the focus of her passion."

"You mean, she'll stop liking Brett and start liking someone else?" Nicole said.

"Precisely. It will work exactly as it did the first time," Mr. Chanter said. "She will smell the smoke of the leaf and fall in love with the next person she sees."

"Why are there two?" I asked.

"In case you mess up the first time," Mr. Chanter said. "You can have a second chance."

"Wow, thanks, Mr. Chanter," I said, reaching for the bag.

But Mr. Chanter quickly hid it behind his back. "I've been thinking, Brett. Don't you think my house needs a new coat of paint?"

"Huh?" I didn't follow.

"I've decided that this summer I'd like you to paint the house and fix all the windows," he said. "You can put in the new lawn *next* summer."

"That's not fair!" I cried. "We made a deal."

"On the other hand," Mr. Chanter said, "I'm sure you'll make a tasty meal for a hungry German shepherd."

He knew he had me. "Okay, Mr. Chanter, you win. I'll paint the house and get the windows fixed this year and do the lawn next year."

"I thought you'd understand." Mr. Chanter handed me the bag of leaves. "Now don't forget. After she smells the smoke, she'll fall in love with the first person she sees."

"Got it, Mr. Chanter. And thanks."

106

I turned to go.

"And, Brett?" Mr. Chanter said.

"Yes?"

"Next time you want some flowers, ask."

"You mean, if I'd asked you would have given them to me?" I said.

"No, but it's still the polite thing to do."

A little while later I dropped Nicole off at Peabody Elementary. "Let me know what happens," she said.

"It's simple, Nicole. If I'm not here to pick you up after school, you'll know what happened."

Nicole looked down and scuffed her foot against the sidewalk. I knew I had to get to school, but I had to say something first.

"You know, I owe you a big thanks," I said. "You really helped me out these last few days. Tell you the truth, I don't know what I would have done without you."

Nicole looked up at me and smiled. Without warning, she rose up on her tiptoes and kissed me on the cheek. I touched my cheek and looked at her, stunned. "Did you sniff the purple flower again?"

Nicole grinned and shook her head. "Not this time, Brett."

I smiled back. "Well, wish me luck."

"Super good luck, Brett."

I started toward the high school.

"Brett?" Nicole said.

I stopped. "Yeah?"

"You know, it wouldn't be the worst thing if you married Julie. I mean, at least we'd get to ride in her car."

"Don't even think about it."

When I got to school, Zack was waiting at my locker.

"You didn't happen to get life insurance, did you?" he asked.

"No," I said. "Is Gary around?"

Zack shook his head. "He said something about having to go to the doctor this morning."

"Okay, then you're going to have to help me," I said. "Come on."

"Where are we going?"

"Over to the senior high side."

Zack stopped. "Are you crazy?"

"You gotta come with me," I said.

"Talk about walking into the jaws of death."

"Let's go," I said.

As we walked over to the senior side, I explained my plan. "I need a place that's totally dark where we can take Julie and not be disturbed."

"That's easy," Zack said. "The darkroom."

"Perfect!" I cried.

We got over to the senior side of school. Everything looked bigger there — the kids, the desks, even the lockers. The high school kids stared at us as we walked down the hall.

"Nothing like feeling welcome," Zack whispered nervously.

Ahead I saw a group of guys hanging around one of the lockers. They were tall and wearing team jackets.

"Uh, excuse me," I said.

The group parted and I found myself facing Trey Boice . . . *and Killer!* The fierce-looking German shepherd had a leather muzzle around his mouth.

Grrrrrr. . . . Killer growled and lunged at Zack and me.

"Ahhhh!" We both screamed and jumped back.

"Down, Killer!" Trey yanked the chain leash and pulled the dog back.

Grrrrr. . . . Killer kept trying to get us, but his paws slipped on the polished tile floor.

I swallowed in terror. "You brought Killer to school to eat me?"

"No," Trey said. "I brought him because Mr. Arnold needs fleas for a science experiment. Eating you is gonna be his reward for being good all morning. So what do you want, Brett?"

"I was wondering if we could talk," I said.

A couple of the guys around Trey smirked.

"Why don't you just feed him to Killer right here," said Adam Lampel.

"Yeah," said Jason Howard. "You'll have a good excuse. You can just say these geeks entered our turf without permission and Killer acted in self-defense."

"I really think we ought to talk," I said.

"About what?" Trey asked.

I motioned for him to step away from his buddies. Trey gave Killer's leash to Adam and came over, scowling.

"This better be good," he mumbled.

"How'd you like to get Julie back?" I asked in a low voice.

Trey glanced back at his buddies to make sure they couldn't hear. "What makes you think I can?" he whispered.

I quickly told him the story of the Amazonian Passion plant and the leaves Mr. Chanter had given me.

"You expect me to believe that?" Trey asked.

"Listen," I said. "Can you think of any other possible reason why Julie would leave *you* for me?"

"Hmmm." Trey scratched his head. "I guess you have a point."

Then I told him the rest of the plan. If everything went well, not only would Trey have Julie back as his girlfriend by the end of lunch, but she'd be his forever.

19

At lunchtime I went to the cafeteria alone. Gary still hadn't come back from his doctor's appointment. Zack was supposed to wait for me and Julie in the darkroom.

Julie, of course, was waiting at my regular table. At tables all around us, kids were watching with amazed looks on their faces.

"Brett," Julie said, looking up at me with that dreamy smile. "You kept your word."

"Uh, yeah."

"I was wondering if you'd like to go to the mall with me after school," she said.

The kids shook their heads in wonder. The prettiest girls in our grade, who usually wouldn't even glance in my direction, were now watching me with fascinated looks on their faces. It wouldn't be easy to give up Julie, but I knew I had to do it.

"I have an idea," I said. "Why don't we go someplace right now where we can be alone?"

"Oh, Brett, I'd love to." Julie got up from the table and slid her arm through mine. The kids started to whisper excitedly.

We left the cafeteria and started down the hall.

"Where are we going?" Julie asked.

"Oh, just a quiet little place I know."

"And we'll be alone?" Julie asked, sort of giggly.

"Pretty much."

"How romantic." I felt her hand slide into mine and squeeze it tightly. "Did I ever tell you how much I admire a man who can be romantic? I think it takes great inner strength and character to be tender and loving."

We reached the darkroom and I stopped. "Uh, well, here we are."

"You want to go in *there*?" Julie asked, her eyes going wide.

I nodded nervously. I was worried that she might refuse to go in a dark place with me.

"Oh, how romantic!" Julie pushed open the door and practically dragged me inside. The door shut behind us and the room went pitch-black. I could smell the developing chemicals in the air.

"Oh, Brett," she cried. "I can't tell you how I've longed for this moment. The two of us together, in the dark, alone."

It was too dark to see anything. *Where was Zack?*

Suddenly a flame burst on.

"What in the — ?" Julie gasped.

In the dim light, I saw a hand hold a leaf over the flame. The leaf caught on fire. A second later I smelled the smoke. That meant Julie must have smelled it, too. I quickly turned Julie around so that she was facing the door.

Right on schedule, the door swung open.

"Hey, Zack, you in here?"

It wasn't Trey!

It was Gary!

"Who . . . who are you?" Julie asked breathlessly.

"Gary Halkit. You haven't seen Zack or Brett, have you?"

But Julie hardly heard him as she stepped close and ran her fingers through his hair. "Gary," she whispered. "What a strong, handsome name."

"Huh?"

Zack reached for the light switch and the room lit up. "Darn," he muttered. "I was kind of hoping she'd see *me* first."

Just then another person appeared in the doorway.

"Am I late?" Trey asked, gasping for breath.

"I'll say," I groaned.

"I couldn't help it," Trey said. "I forgot where the darkroom was."

"Don't tell me," I said. "Tell him." I pointed at Gary, who had backed into the corner to get away from Julie.

"Hey, back off!" he was saying. "I hardly know you."

"What's going on?" Trey looked shocked.

"You were late," I said. "She saw him first."

Trey's jaw dropped. *I'll kill him!*

He lunged at Gary, but Julie spun around and pointed her finger at him. "No, you won't, Trey Boice. You won't touch him!"

Trey staggered backward, seething. He looked so angry I thought his eyes were going to burst out of his head. He fixed his glare on me. "All right!" he shouted. "If I can't kill him, *I'll kill you!*"

"Uh-oh!" I ran out of the darkroom. Outside in the corridor, I saw something that made me freeze in terror.

Adam Lampel was coming down the hall with Killer!

"Give me that dog!" Trey shouted as he came out of the darkroom behind me. He yanked the leash out of Adam's hand and quickly pulled the muzzle off the snarling German shepherd.

"See him, Killer?" Trey yelled, pointing at me as I backed down the hall. "That's lunch!"

"Ahhhhh!" I screamed and started to run. Killer came racing down the hall behind me, growling and barking. I made a quick turn into the corridor where my locker was. Fortunately, my tennis shoes had a better grip on the polished

floors than Killer's paws, and he went sliding past the turn and banged into the wall.

I made it to my locker and quickly started to do the combination. Down the hall, Killer looked dazed as he struggled to his feet.

I fumbled with the combination.

Grrrooooofff! Killer shook his head and came charging down the corridor with his teeth bared.

I pulled on my lock, but it wouldn't open!

Killer was only a dozen yards away now.

I yanked on the lock again.

It opened!

Grrrrrrr! Killer was almost there.

I swung open the locker door.

Killer opened his mouth and bared his sharp teeth.

I grabbed the bouquet of wilted flowers.

Killer lunged at me.

I jammed the flowers into his mouth.

Cruuuunch!

Killer bit the flowers. I quickly hid behind the door of my locker.

"Killer?" Trey ran into the hall. "Where'd that geek go?"

I heard the pitter-patter of paws going down the hall.

"Killer?" Trey sounded puzzled. "What are you doing? Killer? *Killer! Hey, stop it!*"

When I looked out from behind the locker,

Killer had knocked Trey to the ground and was slobbering all over him.

"Stop it, Killer!" Trey cried. *"Stop!"*

But it was no use. Killer was in love.

"Help!" Gary raced around the corner and down the hall toward me. "Brett, she's after me. You gotta help me!"

"Why should I?" I asked.

"Please." Gary grabbed my shirt and begged. "I'll do anything."

"Anything?"

"I swear, anything."

"Gary! Oh, Gary, dearest!" Julie appeared at the end of the hall and came jogging toward us, waving. "Don't run away, my darling!"

Gary looked at me with desperation in his eyes. "What do you say, Brett? Whatever you want, I'll do it."

I smiled. "Fine, I know just what I want you to do."

Meanwhile, Julie was coming closer. "Please wait, Gary. Don't you like me?"

"Ahhhhhh!" Gary took off and ran down the hall.

20

Five Months Later: Summer Vacation

Dressed in T-shirts and shorts, Nicole and I were eating breakfast on the porch.

"I saw Mr. All-County Everything at the mall yesterday with his dog," Nicole said.

"Trey Boice took Killer to the mall?" I asked.

"Killer makes Trey take him everywhere," Nicole said. "He won't let him out of his sight. He won't let anyone near Trey anymore. Not even Julie."

I shook my head in wonder. "Amazing."

"Kids are still talking about how you outwitted Trey," Nicole said. "It's like you're a big hero now."

I had to smile. No one was more surprised than me.

Beep! Beep! We heard the car horn in our driveway.

"Who could that be?" I wondered.

"I'll go see," Nicole said. She went into the kitchen. "It's Julie!"

117

"Serious?"

"Look."

I went to the kitchen and looked out. Julie waved at me. Sitting next to her in the red sports car was Zack. He waved, too. I went out the front door.

"Hey, Brett, me and Julie are going to the beach today," Zack said. "Want to come?"

"Uh, sure," I said. "Just let me go inside and get my stuff."

I went inside.

"So Julie and Zack are still in love," Nicole said.

"Yeah. Ever since we got Julie back into the darkroom and Zack burned that second leaf, she's been crazy about him." I grabbed a bathing suit and towel. "Have a good day at camp."

"Have a great time at the beach." Nicole waved.

I went outside. Zack and Julie were sitting in the car, holding hands.

"Okay, let's go," I said, hopping in.

Instead of backing out of the driveway, Julie pointed over at Mr. Chanter's house. "Isn't that Gary?"

Gary was on a ladder, replacing a broken window on the second floor.

"*Hey, Gary!*" I yelled.

Gary turned and stared at us glumly. "What?"

"How's it going?" Zack said.

"Don't ask," Gary said woefully. "I still have

another hundred windows to fix. It's gonna take me the whole summer."

"Well, take it easy," I said.

"Boy, I can't believe Gary was so scared of Julie that he actually gave her up in exchange for all those jobs at Mr. Chanter's house," Zack said as Julie backed the car out of the driveway.

"I guess some guys just can't handle a serious commitment," I said.

"Does he really have a lot of work to do?" Julie asked.

"Oh, yeah," I said. "After he does all those windows, he's got to paint the house and put in a new lawn. It'll probably take him another two summers."

"It doesn't seem fair," Julie said.

"Hey, what can I tell you?" I said, giving Zack a wink. "As Gary himself would say, 'All's fair in love and war.'"

About the Author

TODD STRASSER is an award-winning author of many novels for young and teenage readers. Among his best known are *Help! I'm Trapped in My Teacher's Body* and *The Mall from Outer Space*. He also wrote Scholastic's novelizations of *Home Alone*™, *Home Alone 2*™, and *Free Willy*.

In addition to writing, Todd Strasser frequently visits elementary and middle schools to speak about writing and conduct writing workshops. Mr. Strasser, who lives in a suburb of New York City, celebrates Valentine's Day each year with his wife and children.